CW01084771

If only, Evelyn would think later: if only there hadn't been the bother in Cuba; if only she'd stayed in London or insisted on going to Amsterdam with her husband; if only she hadn't knocked the Horseman of the Apocalypse and his friend off their motorbike: the week might have turned out very differently.

DAVID GEE

Originally earmarked for the Methodist Mission Field, David Gee discovered that the 'missionary position' didn't suit him. He has worked in telecommunications and journalism in London, Bahrain and Qatar. His previous novels are **Shaikh-Down** and **The Dropout**. He lives on the South Downs outside Brighton.

His website/blog is www.davidgeebooks.com

THE BEXHILL MISSILE CRISIS

– A NOVEL BY –
DAVID GEE

Paradise Press

First published in Great Britain in 2014 by
Paradise Press, BM Box 5700, London WC1N 3XX.
www.paradisepress.org.uk

Copyright © David Gee 2014
www.davidgeebooks.com

The moral right of David Gee to be identified
as the author of this work has been asserted
by him in accordance with the Copyright,
Designs and Patents act 1988.

All rights reserved. No part of this publication
may be reproduced, stored in a retrieval
system, or may be transmitted in any form
or by any means, electronic, mechanical,
photocopying, recording or otherwise, without
the prior permission of the copyright owner.

A CIP catalogue record for this book
is available from the British Library.

ISBN 978 1 904585 59 6

This book is available to download as
an e-book from www.paradisepress.org.uk.

Printed and bound in Great Britain by
Berforts Information Press Ltd, King's Lynn.

Cover photo © David Gee, 2014.

Cover layout and typesetting by Rod Shelton.

for Helen and Roderick
– adeste fideles!

for Colin Spencer

with admiration
– and trepidation!

David Gee
Feb 2014

Author's Note

This is a work of fiction. With the obvious exception of political figures and events in Washington, Moscow and the Caribbean, characters, places and incidents are the product of the author's imagination or are used fictitiously. Any resemblance to actual events, locales or persons, living or dead, is entirely coincidental.

'Sexual intercourse began,' Philip Larkin would have us believe, in 1963 – '*between the end of the* Chatterley *ban and the Beatles' first LP.*' I contend that Larkin was out by one year (although he was probably right about the *Chatterley* effect): sexual intercourse, as we know it, began in 1962. Anyone who was alive at the time of the Cuban 'kerfuffle' will remember the feeling that, with the world on the brink of thermonuclear Armageddon, there might only be time for one last excursion to a favourite location, one last family get-together, one last sexual fling. The four people in *The Bexhill Missile Crisis* don't choose the partner for this fateful fling; he chooses them.

D G

*'It is painful and terrible for me to see
The vile deeds of a great country.'*
Yevgeni Yevtushenko

'Letter to America'
Havana, 24 October 1962

A Visitor's Guide to Bexhill

(Brochure issued by the Town Hall, 1959)

BEXHILL-ON-SEA prides itself on being the cleanest and most salubrious resort on the Sussex coast. An elegant promenade with well-kept lawns and flower-beds makes up two miles of the five-mile sea front.

The most prominent building on the sea front is the 1933 De La Warr Pavilion, one of the finest examples of Art Deco architecture in the country. Designed by Erich Mendelsohn and Serge Chermayeff, it was named in honour of Earl de la Warr, whose family had owned the land around Bexhill since the 12th century.

The Pavilion boasts a bar and tea rooms as well as a theatre in which plays and concerts are performed throughout the summer and a pantomime every winter. Other seafront attractions include a paddling pool, an amusement arcade, and a putting green. For the more serious golfer nearby Cooden Beach has an excellent course which welcomes holiday visitors.

The Parish Church is worth a visit. It is Saxon in origin, albeit much restored over the centuries; a few Norman arches and capitals survive.

The town has excellent shops, cafeterias and restaurants. There are a number of good quality hotels and, for those on a more modest budget, boarding houses offering accommodation on a bed-and-break-fast or half-board basis. Many of these welcome child-ren, although Bexhill's popularity has traditionally been greater with the older visitors who appreciate the town's quietness and flatness.

For the motorist Bexhill, four miles west of Hastings and twelve miles east of Eastbourne, is easily reached from London via the A21 or the A22, in either case continuing on the A259. There are frequent electric trains from Victoria.

MONDAY

'There can be little doubt that something is going on.'

**THE TIMES, 22 October 1962,
reporting on US tension over Cuba**

IN WASHINGTON THE Cuban 'situation', of which the world at large was only today becoming faintly and uneasily aware, had entered its second week.

It was eight days since the discovery by U-2 reconnaissance planes that, ninety miles from Florida, the former hosts of pirates and mobster casino operators were now entertaining Soviet technicians and nuclear missiles with a strike capability against most of the American continent, from Hudson's Bay to the capital of Peru.

For Washington's political and military leaders it had been a week of nerve-wracking debate in the Pentagon, in the State Department and in the Cabinet Room at the White House.

For the unwitting average American citizen a week of lively wrangling over the forthcoming Congressional elections.

For the people of Great Britain a week of prurient speculation about a homosexual Admiralty clerk named William Vassall, on trial at the Old Bailey for offences under the Official Secrets Act.

For fifteen good ladies in the Borough of Bexhill on the Sussex coast a week of fastidious ('pernickety', a bank manager's wife complained to her friend Lillian Rutherford in Hastings) planning for next Saturday's bazaar in aid of Moral Rearmament.

MONDAY OCTOBER 22ND 1962, the eighth day of the Cuban Missile Crisis, was a tense and hectic one for the staff at the White House, the Pentagon and the State Department as they prepared for the President's declaration on national television and radio, at 1900 hours, of the naval 'quarantine' of the ill-starred island.

IN NORTH LONDON'S Hampstead Garden Suburb, Evelyn Hunter, wife of a Bond Street jeweller, pressed clothes and packed her husband's suitcase; he was flying to Amsterdam on Tuesday to stock up on diamonds.

She also ironed and packed for her own five-day trip to Bexhill with Andrew Rutherford, whose business partner was a friend of the Hunters from Sidney's days as a buyer in Selfridges. They were to stay as guests of a divorced friend of Andrew's.

When a 36-year-old married woman is about to spend five days in the country with an unmarried younger man, the question of what she should wear – even when the unmarried younger man is not her lover – assumes more than its usual importance. Evelyn took care to select from her wardrobe sober dresses and cardigans in which she could be confident that her host and his daughter and the virtuous citizens of Bexhill would accept her as a grass widow and not write her off as a society tart.

A sense of unease hung over her all day.

'You're very edgy tonight,' her husband observed at the end of dinner, which they had eaten in near-silence.

'I'm always edgy when you go off on these trips,' she said, aware that her unease had more to do with her impending visit to Bexhill than with Sidney's third trip of the year to Holland. 'I still wish I was coming with you.'

'We've been through all this before,' he reminded her. 'You'd only end up bored to death in the hotel.'

'I could wander around Amsterdam while you meet your dealers.'

They *had* been through this before. Sidney gave a loud sigh. 'You're going to Bexhill,' he said. 'I'm sure you and Andrew will have a nice time at his friend's house.'

Sidney Hunter had no qualms about his wife going away with Andrew. On Sidney's Masonic nights Andrew sometimes took Evelyn out for dinner or a show. Sidney was sure – as was Evelyn – that Andrew entertained no plans to compromise her. They had not failed to notice that the average age of the 'fillies' in his ever-changing stable was not much more than half of hers.

'I suppose we will,' she forced herself to concede. She leaned across to take his dessert plate and stacked it with hers.

'The change of air will do you good. *And* some younger company.'

Evelyn had started to rise. Now she sat down again, taken aback by this line of conversation. 'Why should I need some younger company all of a sudden?'

'Well – I'm such an old fuddy-duddy. You must sometimes wish you had someone a bit more exciting in your life.'

The dessert plates rattled as Evelyn let them drop back onto her tablemat. 'Don't you *dare* say that. I've never regretted choosing you and don't you ever think otherwise.'

'All right, lovie. I'm sorry.' He rose and moved round the dining table to kiss her cheek. She patted his head, ruffling the thin hair. Then he went to turn the television on in the living half of the room while she took the dishes out to the kitchen, wondering if – and if so, why – he shared her apprehensions about the visit to Bexhill.

ANDREW RUTHERFORD LEFT his packing for Tuesday morning. He spent a normal busy Monday at his company's offices in Mayfair, a display and artwork agency established, with Sidney Hunter's backing, eighteen months ago which now employed a staff of four and provided Sidney with a good return on his investment.

After work he had a drink in a local pub with his agency partner Algernon Farley – 'Algie' – who was fifty-five to Andrew's twenty-four. At 6.15 he met his nineteen-year-old girlfriend Fiona – *Lady* Fiona Camelford-Jones – outside Swan & Edgar's and took her to dine at Quaglino's. After dinner they went back to Andrew's penthouse flat in South Kensington where Fiona duly sang for the supper he'd given her.

'Will your friend Mrs Hunter be getting some of this while you're in Sussex?' she asked as she began dressing. Even stepping into coral-pink knickers, Lady Fiona managed to look ladylike. In September she had accompanied Andrew to a cocktail party in Hampstead Garden Suburb. Fiona thought – and said – that the Hunters and their neighbours were suburban (a geographical fact) and Jewish (which was only true of five of the fourteen guests). Whatever opinion the Hunters formed of Fiona, they kept it to themselves, as did Lillian, Andrew's mother, when she was introduced over a restaurant dinner in Knightsbridge.

'Mrs Hunter's not that sort of friend,' he replied, lying in a black silk dressing gown on top of the bed-clothes.

'I think she'd like to be.' She fastened her suspender belt.

'Older woman, younger man. That's a bit Somerset

Maugham, wouldn't you say?'

Perching on the edge of the bed she drew on the first of her stockings. 'My parents tell me I sat on his lap once as a baby, when they were in Malaya.' She snapped on the stocking. 'Did you know he was a queer?'

'Yes, I did.' He reached for a cigarette as she pulled up the other stocking.

'*You're* like a character out of Maugham, Andrew. A bit dated. Always striking poses. Madly in love with yourself.'

On these criteria Noël Coward would be a more apt comparison, Andrew thought, but he kept this to himself. Instead he asked: 'What's brought this on? Are you peeved that I'm going to Bexhill with Mrs Hunter? Or did my performance tonight fail to bring satisfaction?'

'I couldn't care less who you go away with – to Bexhill or anywhere else.' Her brassiere lay on the floor and she bent down to pick it up. 'But since you ask, Jocelyn and I are agreed that you're only a four-star performer.'

He grimaced. 'I know you two were in school together, but I hadn't realized that you compare notes over a scorecard.'

'Ever since Roedean.' Her fingers briskly buttoned a white nylon blouse. White on white. Fiona never sunbathed; her skin was porcelain, but not flawless: knees and shins bore indentations from school hockey injuries. Andrew's skin had the look of tan leather; he'd spent the first ten days of October in Positano. 'Of course it was girls then.'

'And I only rate four stars? I'm crushed.'

She wriggled into a knee-length navy-blue skirt, her salesgirl uniform in Harrods (debt and divorce, post-Malaya, had lowered the Camelford-Jones standard of living). 'We give three to a man who takes good care of himself and four to a man who takes good care of us.'

'And five to the one who does both, I presume?'

'Right.' she said, splashing her neck from one of his bottles of aftershave. 'But it takes a real man to do that.'

'Which, in the view of this tribunal, I am not.'

'You try a little too hard to please.' She returned to the bed and bent over to kiss his forehead. 'Next time think of yourself a bit more. Not too much, of course. We wouldn't want you to turn into a rugby player.' She left the bedroom with a cavalier wave. Moments later he heard the front door click shut.

Lying on the white silk bedspread in his black silk robe, Andrew frowned. If he had to put a name to his image of himself, it would be 'Byronic'. 'Maughamish' definitely wouldn't do. If he were to discuss Fiona's rating system with Algie (who was what Fiona called 'a queer'), Algie would purse his lips and say something like: 'You'll have to butch yourself up a bit, darling'.

'Butch' wasn't Andrew's style – any more than it had been Byron's. Byron must have had many girls like Fiona in his life. And, quite possibly, a friend like Algie.

EVELYN CLOSED HER library book in the middle of a chapter, unable to concentrate. She fought down the desire for a cigarette. Only a light smoker himself, Sidney hated her to smoke in bed and was grumpy if he woke in the morning with the smell of tobacco in the room. Tonight he'd taken one of Evelyn's sleeping pills to calm the nervousness he always felt before flying. Now he snored asthmatically on his back beside her.

The bald patch at the back of his head shone in the lamplight, a droll symbol of the durability of their union. When Evelyn had first known him in 1945, thirty-two to her nineteen, he'd had a full head of hair which had barely begun to recede by the time of their wedding two years later.

You must sometimes wish you had someone a bit more exciting in your life, she repeated to herself and immediately – ridiculously – remembered the thirty-year-old German who'd clumsily courted her in a Torquay hotel two years ago (Sidney in Holland again). In the lamplight Evelyn looked again at her 49-year-old husband's balding pate and pictured in its place the German's head with its thick black mane. If What-was-his-name? were here now, at eleven forty-something, would he be snoring into the pillow, or would his blunt fingers be probing her parted thighs while she arched her breasts into his face, sighing and moaning?

She sighed a different sigh from the one in her mind. She hadn't married for excitement fifteen years ago, she'd married for comfort and security, and comfort and security was what she had got. It was too late, now, for excitement, too late for passion, too late for ecstasy.

Evelyn turned out the light and slithered down into the bed. She wrapped one arm round her husband's body, embracing the familiar warmth of his flabby stomach, and tried to sleep.

AFTERWARDS, WHEN IT was all over, Evelyn would convince herself that her unease, the 'edginess' her husband had noticed, had been a *premonition* of the Crisis that was about to break – the global one in Cuba and her personal crisis in Bexhill.

IN LONDON IT was almost midnight. In Washington it was approaching seven p.m.

At the State Department a group of ambassadors from America's allies, shocked and shaken after a briefing by Undersecretary George Ball, was gathering in front of a television set for the President's speech. As they waited a savings and loan company's commercial appeared on the screen, earnestly demanding of the unseen and unforeseeing audience:

'*How much security does your family have?*'

A ripple of laughter momentarily exploded the tension in the briefing room. Then, as the picture gave way to the seal of office of the President of the United States, the group of men seemed to draw breath together.

TUESDAY

'It will be most difficult to keep such a business on a local scale. We can only pray nevertheless that this can be done.'

**DAILY TELEGRAPH editorial,
23 October 1962**

MORNING

IF ONLY, EVELYN would think later: if only there hadn't been the bother in Cuba; if only she'd stayed in London or insisted on going to Amsterdam with her husband; if only she hadn't knocked the Horseman of the Apocalypse and his friend off their motorbike: the week might have turned out very differently.

'PRESIDENT KENNEDY'S ANNOUNCEMENT last night of a naval blockade of Cuba until Soviet missiles on the island are dismantled and removed has sent a shockwave round the world. At the United Nations in New York ...'

Turning the radio down, Sidney forked bacon and egg into his mouth.

'Well – obviously you're not going to Holland,' Evelyn said.

'I can't think why not.'

'But – this is going to be World War Three.'

'Listen to what they're saying,' he instructed her, although their conversation was drowning the radio commentary. 'This is going to be a war of *words*. A few threats, a bit of bluffing, then they'll find a face-saving compromise and it'll all blow over.' He smiled mollifyingly. 'Honestly, lovie, they're not going to start firing missiles at each other.' He reloaded his fork. 'And I've got a business to run.'

'How can you think of business at a time like this?' she said. Sidney shook his head and brought the fork to his mouth. Evelyn wanted to shake *him*. 'Anyway, I'm definitely coming with you now,' she went on. If she was with him, somehow there would be less danger, or no danger that she couldn't face.

'No you're not,' he said, still chewing.

'But I want to be with you – just in case – you know ...' She broke off, discouraged by his expression. She knew him in this mood: he wouldn't give in. 'Anyway,' she ventured again, conceding only a partial defeat, 'I shall phone Andrew when I get back from the airport and tell him I'm *not* going to Bexhill.'

Sidney's hand, holding the fork, hit the table with a bang that rattled the crockery.

LAURENCE LET FLY with the shotgun. A dozen gulls took off shrieking from the fence that separated the garden from the thirty-foot drop to the beach. Two rooks abandoned their scratching at the soil against a plaited willow windbreak and flapped into the watery-blue sky.

An agitated face appeared at the kitchen window as Laurence walked up the paving stones towards the house.

'Oh Mr Dickinson, I wish you'd warn us before you let that thing off. We thought they'd started a war.'

Laurence laughed. 'I don't think the kerfuffle in Washington is likely to lead to an invasion of Sussex, Mrs Danvers, but if it does, you and Cook will be in for rather more than a few shotgun pellets.'

The housekeeper withdrew, sniffing huffily, from the window. Her real name was Ormsby-Lowndes; Andrew had renamed her three years ago: the double-barrelled name was, he said, an embarrassing reminder that the venerable line into which she had married had been reduced to keeping house for the Dickinsons who'd come up from nothing and were inclined to marry bar-maids.

Laurence mounted the steps to the terrace. Beyond the conservatory his eighteen-year-old daughter stood beside a rattan cane chair mopping at her floral print dress with a paper napkin. The sea breeze ruffled her long honey-coloured hair. It was a constant mystery to Laurence that he and Louise could ever have managed to produce anything so petite and exquisite as Sarah. He was a big man, not tall but broad-shouldered and heavily built, running to fat at forty-five; and Louise's charms had always been similarly on the substantial side. She looked up as he approached.

'Laurence, must you keep blasting away with that bloody thing? Look at my sodding dress.'

'*Sodden*, dear. The word for wet is sodden.'

'It wasn't a word for wet I wanted.'

Laurence rested the shotgun against the conservatory wall. A single-barrelled Abercrombie & Fitch 12-gauge, he had bought it from a farmer at his golf club who'd upgraded to something more lethal to protect his chickens from foxes. 'My poor roses will never stand a chance with those rooks,' Laurence said, sitting down in the other chair.

Sarah crouched down to wipe her left foot and ankle. 'No one in their right mind tries to grow outdoor roses in winter within fifty yards of the English Channel.'

'I really don't think that horticulture is a sphere on which you can speak with any authority, dear child.'

'Well, up yours, Daddy darling.'

Laurence picked up the half-empty tumbler from the glass-topped table beside his chair and sniffed its contents. 'If you must drink Coca-Cola, I think you ought to drink it without rum at least some of the time, Sarah. We don't want to end up like Louise, do we? And it's a bit tactless to be drinking *Cuba libre* today of all days.'

Sarah stood up and relieved him of her glass. 'I hope we aren't going to talk politics all week.'

'I shouldn't think so. Politics has never rated very

high in Andrew's interests.'

'What about this new mistress of his?'

'For God's sake, Sarah. I've told you already: Mrs Hunter's husband is Andrew's backer. I think we can reasonably assume that she is *not* Andrew's mistress. I believe he's still got that girlfriend he brought down here last year.'

'But now he's bringing this married woman. Where's her husband?'

'Mr Hunter's going to Holland to see some diamond merchants.'

'Oh well, if her husband's in the diamond business, I guess she knows which side her bread is buttered on.'

Laurence sighed. 'There's your mother coming out in you again.'

'God bless her and keep her in California.' Sarah raised her glass in a toast to her distant mother, then drained it and set it down. 'Well, I'm off to Ruth's for some tennis.'

'All right, dear. Have fun. And remember to lose graciously.'

'Who says I'm going to lose?'

'I meant, *if* you lose.'

'No fear of that.' She entered the house via the conservatory. Laurence watched her go with a smile. He always enjoyed their bantering exchanges which teetered on but never crossed the line into bickering. Not for the first time he thanked God that she'd chosen to live with him after she started boarding school and that her mother hadn't contested the decision. A teenage daughter, even one as pretty as Sarah, might have proved an encumbrance in Louise's relentless climb up the social and marital ladders of England, Italy and, currently, the United States. The barmaid from Hastings had gone a long way since her Rita Hayworth glamour turned the head of a lonely sailor on shore leave in 1943 and Laurence also continued to thank God for being left far behind in her wake.

He picked up the shotgun and went indoors to change out of his gardening clothes into something more suitable for receiving guests.

AFTERNOON

THE ACCIDENT, EVELYN would decide afterwards, was Andrew's fault. If only (another '*if only*') he hadn't distracted her, made her nervous, blathering on about his girlfriend's fake orgasms ...

'THIS IS A TERRIBLY narrow road,' she said. Accustomed to the Finchley Road and the avenues of Hampstead Garden Suburb, Evelyn drove her Renault at a near-crawling pace along the rural lane with its steep high-hedged bank and treacherous mulch of fallen leaves. 'I wish we'd stayed on the A21.'

'This is England's green and pleasant land we're in now,' he told her. 'Or perhaps, seeing as it's autumn, *brown* and pleasant. You're supposed to feel a stirring in your loins. Talking of which, d'you know I think I caught Fiona faking an orgasm last night.'

'Do we really have to discuss your sex life while I'm driving?'

'Yes, Evelyn, I'm afraid we must.'

'This is the Fiona you brought to our dinner party?'

'I know she behaved appallingly. It's not easy being upper-class and highly strung.'

'She said Sid and I were suburban. He has a shop in *Bond* Street!'

'Yes, but your house is practically outside the North

Circular. Anyway, last night, there we were on my best sheets after a nice dinner at Quaglino's. Fiona's hitting more top C's than Joan Sutherland on a good night and clawing my back with her nails, and I could swear she was checking the time on her wristwatch over my shoulder. The watch is a Cartier, needless to say.'

'I hear enough about Cartier at home, thank you,' said Evelyn.

'Of course you do. Forgive me, darling.'

She wished he wouldn't call her 'darling' all the time. 'I wish –' she started to say, but he interrupted her:

'Tell me honestly, Evelyn, do you ever fake orgasms with Sid? Or with anybody else, for that matter.'

'Andrew!' She went scarlet and turned to him with an outraged expression, then quickly turned her head back to the road as a banked hedge-lined curve opened to an unannounced crossroads and events began to happen faster than she could control them.

'Do I – oh my God!'

'Look out, darling.'

The motorcycle seemed to appear from nowhere and with no warning engine roar which, in a soft-topped car, she would surely have heard. Coming fast from the right it skidded across the junction with a sudden screech of brakes. Evelyn stamped on the Renault's brakes and swerved hard, but her front bumper struck the rear wheel of the cycle a glancing blow. On the other side of the crossroads the verge was flatter and lower; brambles overhung a ram-shackle fence with a wood beyond it. The motorbike spun onto the verge with a jolt that catapulted the pillion passenger into the saplings bordering the wood. The motorcyclist gave a yell as his machine piled heavily into the brambles. Fence timbers cracked.

The Renault stalled in the middle of the junction.

Evelyn put it in neutral and yanked on the handbrake. 'Oh my God,' she said again.

Andrew opened his door. 'Stay here.'

'Don't be silly.' She started to get out. 'I did St John Ambulance work in the war. I'm likely to be more useful than you are.'

He steadied her with his hand as she stumbled onto the verge.

'I hope they're all right,' she said.

'I hope Sid's kept your insurance up to date.'

The cyclist detached himself from his machine and the brambles and vaulted the fence at a point where it had been partly flattened at a break in the bushes. Andrew assisted Evelyn over the collapsed section of fence. Her low heels lurched on the soft woodland soil as they hurried to where the cyclist was kneeling over the body of his passenger.

He looked up as they approached, the woman who'd run him down, a small auburn-haired thirty-plus woman in a dark-blue linen dress, and her companion, a tall slim dark-haired younger man in a cream-coloured linen suit.

The motorcyclist was about the same age as Andrew but stockily built, dressed in a black leather jacket and blue jeans. His pale-skinned face, scratched by thorns, was full and fleshy under tightly-curled reddish-blond hair. Dark eyes stared coldly up at the two arrivals.

Evelyn crouched down and began to run her fingers gently over the limbs of the boy on the ground.

'Don't touch him,' the cyclist said. His voice was quiet and controlled, lacking both accent and inflexion.

'I know what I'm doing,' Evelyn said. 'I've had some training in first aid.' She moved her hands slowly across the boy's chest, feeling his ribs. The cyclist made no move to stop her. A trickle of blood from one of his cuts ran under the collar of his jacket. His expression, as he raised his eyes to Andrew standing over Evelyn, held a hint of scorn.

On his back among the withered leaves, legs flat together, the boy looked like a corpse, neatly laid out. He was perhaps eighteen or younger, short and slender with a pale narrow face and straight black hair. Like the other he was dressed in leather and denim. There was no sign of blood or visible injury, but he lay utterly still, eyes closed, his breathing inaudible; only the faint rise and fall of his chest betrayed that he was not in fact dead. A leaf fluttered down and settled on his stomach. Evelyn brushed it off. She felt his neck and jaw, then explored his skull with her fingertips.

'I don't think he's broken anything,' she said. 'Of course he might be injured internally. He seems to be concussed.' She glared across the inert form at the cyclist. 'Why don't you wear crash helmets?'

He met her eyes unblinkingly but made no reply.

'Can we get him to the car?' Andrew said.

'I think we should call an ambulance. Will you take the car and look for a phone.'

'You forget that I don't drive.'

'Then *I'll* have to go. You'd better come with me, in case I get lost.' She stood up. 'Don't move him,' she said to the cyclist who still knelt on the other side of the body. His scratches had begun to congeal into uneven streaks of dark red on his pallid skin. Bending forward, he took the boy's head in his large hands, spreading his fingers as if he would crush the skull beneath them. With his leather jacket and blood-streaked face, he looked to Evelyn like some Wild Man of the Woods crouched over the unconscious body intending perhaps to wrench its head off. 'What are you doing?' she demanded.

The boy's eyes opened.

'My-oh-my,' Andrew murmured. 'Do you have any other tricks, like driving out demons?' He smirked, but

Evelyn found herself shuddering. The boy struggled into a sitting position, assisted by his companion with an arm about his shoulders.

'Careful,' Evelyn warned. 'Are you all right?' she asked the boy.

He managed a fleeting smile.

'Do you hurt anywhere?'

He shook his head.

'Are you sure?'

He nodded solemnly.

'Why doesn't he say something?' Andrew asked.

'He doesn't speak,' the cyclist said.

'Is he lip-reading?'

'He's not deaf. He just doesn't speak, that's all.'

'Are you sure you feel all right?' Evelyn asked the boy, who answered with another smile. His teeth were like a child's: small, white, uneven. He stood up and began to dust the leaves off his clothes.

'We'd better get back to the car,' Evelyn said, 'before somebody runs into it and we have another accident to contend with.' She supported herself once more on Andrew's arm as they walked back to the gap in the bushes, the cyclist following with the boy.

Jammed upright between two bars of the fence, the motorbike was an old machine, the engine casing dented and dirty. A guitar, undamaged, was strapped between two panniers at the rear. The cyclist untied the instrument and handed it to his passenger.

'Who's the musician?' Andrew enquired.

'He is.'

'And what do you do?'

'I sing.'

'Is this a professional partnership?'

'You could say so.'

As he heaved the machine free of the fence, the exhaust pipe came partially away. Thorns had ripped the front tyre; the rusty mudguard was buckled.

Straddling the machine, the cyclist kicked down on the starter. Nothing happened. He kicked again, harder. The exhaust pipe came off completely.

Andrew laughed. 'Looks as if we owe you a new bike.'

'My insurance will cover it,' Evelyn added.

'It's not worth a claim,' the cyclist said with a shrug. 'It was nearly done for. We were going to dump it at Dover.' His voice, as he made this his most informative speech so far, remained uninflected, strangely mechanical. Perhaps, Evelyn thought, he didn't do much talking to his mute companion. It was difficult to picture him as some sort of pop or folk singer. The boy's recovery had not allayed her sense of something sinister, menacing, about the cyclist. As if she felt herself threatened, Evelyn moved closer to Andrew.

'Are you planning to do your act abroad?' Andrew asked.

'Yes: why not?'

'Why not indeed.'

'You must at least let us give you some money for your fares,' Evelyn offered. Even though it was her car, her driving, that had created this mess, she felt that she would hand over every last penny in her handbag to be rid of them.

'There's no need for that. We can hitchhike.'

'Well, anyway,' Andrew said, 'we can give you a lift into Bexhill.'

The cyclist shrugged again. 'Okay.' He turned to the Renault. 'Nice-looking car,' he said with his first show of animation.

'It's a Renault Floride,' Evelyn told him. 'Not much room with Andrew's case in the back,' she apologized. 'The boot's full with my stuff.'

'If you take the top off, he and I can ride on the back.' He waved a hand towards the boy, standing in the road with the guitar.

'We can make room for him to sit in the car properly,' Andrew said.

While he and Evelyn folded back the roof, the other pair removed from the motorcycle the two panniers which presumably held all their possessions. The cyclist wheeled the clattering machine through the break in the bushes and abandoned it inside the wood. Turning Andrew's suitcase on its end they squeezed the panniers into the space behind the driving seat. Andrew nursed Evelyn's mink coat on his lap. The boy settled into the seat behind Andrew with another smile, nursing the guitar. The cyclist sat casually on the back with his legs either side of the boy as they set off. The road left the wood. Now there were houses on each side, new-looking houses and bungalows with well-kept gardens. Evelyn drove at a careful pace.

Turning round, Andrew introduced himself and Evelyn. The boy smiled out from behind Evelyn's seat.

'I'm Pilgrim and he's Malcolm,' the cyclist said.

'Pilgrim,' Andrew repeated. 'Don't you have a first name?'

'I just call myself Pilgrim.'

'Well, we've rather hindered your progress!'

The cyclist had a full-lipped mouth; his smile was merely a brief narrowing of his lips; he did not show his teeth.

'Andrew, there's a roundabout ahead. It says left for Bexhill.'

'Go straight over, darling. We don't need to go through the town. Do you come from around here?' he asked Pilgrim.

'No.'

'Do you know the area at all?'

'I know Hastings.'

'We're going to stay with a friend of mine in Bexhill. He has a hotel in Hastings. In fact he owns several hotels on this part of the coast. I hope you're not a communist.'

'I believe in the survival of the fittest.'

Evelyn recalled what she had thought as he crouched over the boy in the woods. 'That's the law of the jungle,' she said.

'It works for the jungle,' Pilgrim said.

'Not a communist, anyway,' said Andrew. 'Have you heard about what's happening in Cuba?'

'I saw the headlines in somebody's paper.'

'I had a job to get Evelyn out of London. She wanted to hide in the cellar in case Russian missiles start falling.'

'Andrew, I did not!' she protested, reddening.

'Not much protection from missiles in a cellar,' Pilgrim said.

'My view exactly,' said Andrew. 'Eat, drink and be merry, et cetera.'

The road climbed a hill, passing trim little cottages and mansion-sized houses, then descended to a golf course and Cooden Beach station. A bridge carried the railway over the road.

'Oh look, there's the sea,' Evelyn exclaimed.

'Yes, darling. Left at the roundabout.'

Evelyn turned her head to check on Malcolm as she slowed for the roundabout. He gave an impish grin. She glanced up at Pilgrim, who met her gaze expressionlessly, bracing himself now with his hands as well as his feet. She suppressed another shudder.

Beyond the roundabout fifty yards of shingle sloped down to a wider expanse of sand. The tide was on the turn. Low rippling waves encroached slowly on the glistening sand. Half a mile out a yacht turned into the wind, its white sail fluttering. Some children were playing on the sand. Two elderly women chatted on a bench. The sun shone weakly. There had been fog at Heathrow this morning, but here it was a mild afternoon, almost warm.

'Doesn't look much like Armageddon, does it?'
Andrew commented.

'It's lovely,' Evelyn said. 'Don't say such things.'
She pressed down on the accelerator and the view of
the sea was lost behind the first of the houses on the
low cliff that began after the exposed stretch of beach
at the roundabout.

A few minutes later Andrew directed her into the
gravelled drive of a large house with a timbered façade
and elaborate brickwork. A garage with rooms above it
was set to the rear of the house on its left side, flanked
by greenhouses and a garden shed.

'What a beautiful house,' Evelyn said. 'Is it genuine
Tudor?'

'1930s fake. Quite a good fake, if you like that sort
of thing, which Laurence obviously does.'

'And you obviously don't. Shall I stop here?' She
did anyway, parking beside the main entrance. The
front door opened and Laurence came down the two
broad shallow steps. Introductions and Andrew's
account of the incident in the wood were brought to a
sudden conclusion when Malcolm slumped against the
side of the car; he would have fallen onto the gravel
had Pilgrim not moved to catch him. Laurence quickly
led them into the oak-panelled entrance hall where the
housekeeper was waiting.

'Phone the doctor,' said Laurence. 'Quickly. This
lad's been in an accident.'

Pilgrim set Malcolm down on a brown-velvet chaise
longue. Evelyn knelt on a Persian rug beside the
couch, took the boy's pulse and felt his neck and chest
for an injury she might have overlooked in the wood.
Pilgrim sat on an oak chest near the front door and
began to roll a cigarette. Laurence and Andrew stood
at the head of the couch.

'Sorry to dump this on your doorstep,' Andrew said.

'My dear chap, it can't be helped.' He turned to

Pilgrim. 'Are *you* all right?'

'Just a few scratches.'

'We'll get those seen to as soon as we've sorted out your young friend.'

Evelyn looked up anxiously. 'I can't think what can be wrong with him,' she said.

'It's probably only concussion,' Laurence suggested. 'If it was anything more serious I don't think he'd have come round in the first place.'

'Concussion can be serious enough,' Evelyn said.

The housekeeper returned with the information that the doctor was on his way. Laurence instructed her to take Mrs Hunter to her room.

'Oh, but I ought to stay with him,' Evelyn protested.

'The doctor lives close by,' Laurence said. 'He'll be here in a minute or two. I really think you should lie down for a while. You look all in.'

'He's right,' said Andrew. 'Go on, Mrs Danvers, take her away.'

The housekeeper led Evelyn up the broad flight of stairs to the first floor.

'Poor Evelyn,' Andrew said. 'She's in a complete funk about this Cuba business, which she thinks I don't take seriously enough.'

'Oh well,' said Laurence, 'she'll find a soulmate in Mrs D. If she had her way I'd be digging up my rose garden to build a nuclear shelter!'

They looked down at the boy stretched out on the couch, eyes closed, a whisper of breath issuing from his parted lips. 'Cute little thing, isn't he?' Andrew said softly.

'Isn't he,' Laurence echoed. Across the hall his eyes met Pilgrim's. Pilgrim held his gaze until Laurence looked away.

EVERYTHING IN THE room was blue, from the dark-on-light-blue striped wallpaper to the indigo veneer of the wardrobe and dressing table. The window overlooked the terrace and the lawn running down to the cliff. Evelyn leaned against the royal-blue velvet curtains.

'Would you like an aspirin, Mrs Hunter?'

Evelyn turned. 'I don't think I need anything, thank you, Mrs – is your name really the same as the house-keeper in *Rebecca*?'

The other woman smiled. There were grey streaks in her hair, which was drawn in a tight bun, but her face was ruddy and unlined.

'It's a joke of Mr Andrew's from when he lived here. Are you sure you won't come and lie down?'

'Perhaps I will,' Evelyn said. She crossed the room and lay on the bed, kicking off her shoes. 'I hope that boy's going to be all right.'

'I'm sure he will be. You mustn't make yourself nervous.'

'I've been in a state since breakfast,' Evelyn confessed. 'This situation in Cuba's got me worried stiff. But Andrew tells me I'm overreacting and my husband's gone off to Amsterdam on business as if this is just a normal week.'

The housekeeper straightened a doily on the bedside table. 'Mr Dickinson's the same. He says the politicians have to blow hot air every now and then to justify their existence.' She sighed. 'Ah well, like my mother used to say: it's the women who worry while the men go off and make wars.'

'Please God it never comes to that again,' Evelyn said.

'Amen,' the housekeeper added solemnly. Dimly there came the sound of a car door slamming. 'That'll be the doctor,' she said.

LAURENCE OPENED THE front door.

'Hello, young man. Your patient's in here.'

'Good afternoon, Mr Dickinson.' Carrying a worn

Gladstone bag, the doctor entered. He was a man of
Andrew's age with a rugby-player's broad build like
Laurence and fair crinkly hair. 'My father's playing golf,
so I' – he broke off. 'Good lord: *Andrew*!'

'Hello, David. Long time no see. Have you come
back to Sussex?'

'No, we're still in Surrey but my wife's due to have
our second baby any day now, and we thought it would
be nice to have this one down here, so I've taken some
holiday. Anyway' – he crossed the hall – 'I'd better
have a look at this lad.' He bent down and lifted Malcolm's eyelids.

'How long has David's father been your doctor?'
Andrew asked Laurence.

'A couple of years. He took over old Parris's
practice when he retired. Did he used to be your GP in
Hastings? Is that how you and David know each
other?'

'David and I were at school together,' Andrew said,
watching the doctor who had unbuttoned Malcolm's
shirt and was gently feeling his ribs. The pale flesh of
the boy's chest was thickly matted with black hairs.

'It's a small world,' Laurence said. He winced as
Pilgrim stubbed his cigarette into the soil of a copper-
potted aspidistra. 'David's sister and Sarah are a
formidable doubles team at the local tennis club.'

'They're playing now,' David said. 'On my parents'
court.' He stood up. 'May I use your phone, Mr
Dickinson? I'd better call an ambulance. I think it's just
concussion, but I need to have him X-rayed.'

Laurence gestured towards a door on the left.
'There's a phone in the study.' As the doctor crossed to
the door, another car entered the drive with a roar of
acceleration. It squealed to a halt, gravel thrown up by
its tyres rattling on the farthest of the hall windows.
Moments later Sarah came into the hall, followed by
another girl in a tennis skirt, a pimply brunette. Andrew

crossed to them.

'Sarah.' He brought her hand to his lips. '*Je suis ravi.*'

She giggled. 'Ooh, Laurence. I'm getting a flash-back to Charles.'

'"Sharlz",' Andrew mimicked. ''Oo eez zees "Sharlz"?'

'A lost boyfriend of Sarah's from Aix-en-Provence,' Laurence explained. 'Be gentle with her. She's nursing a broken heart.'

'Rhubarb to you, Daddy dear.'

Andrew tut-tutted. 'Children have no respect for their elders any more, do they?' He turned to the dark-haired girl and kissed her hand gravely. 'Ruth. I fear you've forgotten me. You were barely out of nappies when we last saw each other.'

'I don't think so,' she said. Her voice had a slight lisp. 'I remember you and David were always off some-where on your bikes.' She gestured at Malcolm. 'Is he hurt badly?'

'Your brother thinks it's concussion,' Laurence said.

David returned from the study. 'Ambulance is on its way,' he announced. He walked over to Pilgrim and lifted his chin with one hand. 'Have you got anything apart from these cuts?'

Pilgrim held up his hands which were also scratched.

'Can I do something?' Ruth offered.

'You could clean up this young man's cuts and grazes, if you like.' He returned to Malcolm, kneeling to take the boy's pulse again. Ruth crossed to Pilgrim. 'Have you got some TCP in your bag, David?' Her brother shook his head.

'There's some in my bathroom cabinet,' Sarah said.

'Ruth's going into nursing,' Laurence informed Andrew.

'They're a dedicated family.'

'Ruth's going to specialize in *private* nursing,' Sarah said. 'She's hoping to marry a rich invalid.'

'Oh, that's not true,' Ruth protested, colouring.

'Sarah's mother could give you some coaching,' Andrew told her. 'How *is* the lush – I mean, *luscious* Louise?' he asked Laurence.

'Drinking heavily, we assume. She's between husbands – again.'

'Come upstairs,' Ruth instructed Pilgrim, the lisp less noticeable as her voice assumed a businesslike tone. She ushered him towards the staircase, Sarah following.

'Don't worry about your friend,' Laurence called after them. 'I'm sure he'll be all right.'

Pilgrim stopped and looked down at the three men grouped around the chaise longue. He nodded, then turned and mounted the stairs between the two girls.

LYING ON THE royal-blue satin bedspread in her navy-blue linen dress Evelyn felt in danger of fading into the décor.

Her week in Bexhill had hardly got off to a good start. She hoped, prayed, that she hadn't caused Malcolm any serious injury. He was a sweet-looking boy, or maybe that was because he could only communicate with smiles. There was nothing sweet about his companion. The thought of Pilgrim made her skin crawl.

She replayed the accident in her mind. Why had Andrew asked that extraordinary, outrageous question? How dare he assume that she was interested in the details of his sex life and eager to exchange her own marital secrets! Now look what it had led to.

Of course the accident had let her off the hook. How would she have answered his question? Whatever reply she'd made, he would have teased her mercilessly. Just thinking about it, lying on the blue bed in her blue dress, she blushed.

A succession of car doors slammed distantly.

DAVID WENT WITH Malcolm in the ambulance. Half-an-hour later he telephoned to report that the boy had come to again in the X-ray room. There were no fractures or internal injuries, but he would be kept in for observation. Pilgrim was required to fill in forms and David wanted Ruth to fetch him home in his car. Laurence relayed the news to the others in the conservatory where tea had been served.

'I'll run you to the hospital,' Sarah said to Pilgrim. The scratches on his face were less visible following Ruth's ministrations. She had bandaged his left hand. As the trio left the conservatory, the housekeeper came in with a fresh pot of tea.

'We can put that young man over the garage till his friend's fit to travel,' Laurence told her.

'But what will we do if your new chauffeur turns up?'

'I don't think he's going to, but if he does we've got room in the house. Sit down and have some tea with Andrew, Mrs D., while I phone the police station about Mrs Hunter's little mishap with the motorbike.'

'GREAT CAR,' PILGRIM said, settling into the front passenger seat of Laurence's Bentley. 'It must be the next best thing to a Rolls.'

'According to my father a Bentley is as good as a Rolls and a lot less showy,' Sarah said, starting up. 'Anyway, it's more fun than going in my old Morris Minor.' She beat Ruth out of the drive in David's Ford Prefect.

THE LOCAL POLICE superintendent was a member of Laurence's golf club.

'I can't see a need for us to prosecute a charge of

careless driving,' he said, 'unless of course the young man in hospital turns out to have sustained a serious injury. But we will require a formal report of the accident for the record, if you could arrange for the parties involved to come to the station and give their statements.'

'Will tomorrow do?'

'Tomorrow will be fine.'

'WHAT'S THIS ABOUT a new chauffeur?' Andrew demanded as soon as the housekeeper left them alone. 'I wasn't aware you had an old one.' He lit a mentholated cigarette.

'I don't. And I'm not sure I've got this one. He's Italian. *Half*-Italian, actually. Italian father, English mother. He was singing in a restaurant in Sitges when I was out there last month looking at a hotel I might buy.'

'Are Dickinson Hotels going international now?'

'They may be. Mass tourism's really taking off all along that coast.'

'Surely you're not going into the package tour trade?'

'Don't be such a snob, Andrew. It's a growth industry – and a sight more respectable than all those adulterous dirty-weekenders in my hotels in Hastings and Brighton.'

'Respectability isn't what bothers me. Tell me more about your singing chauffeur.'

Laurence coloured slightly. 'He's a year younger than you. His name's Carlo Marini. I had a couple of drinks with him, and then a dinner, and I ended up inviting him to come here when they lay him off. I thought he could sing in my Brighton hotel – drum up some business for the bar and dining room during the quiet season ...'

'Serenading your dirty-weekenders, you mean?'

Laurence laughed. 'Whoever. And I said he could

do a bit of driving as well – not that I need a chauffeur.'

Andrew gave him a challenging look. 'Any other little duties you have in mind for him?'

Laurence's colour deepened. 'Not the kind of thing you're thinking of. Oddly enough, he reminds me more than a bit of you.'

'As *I* used to remind you of someone else. This sounds like the recipe for another romantic disaster, Laurence old fruit.'

The other smiled and shook his head. 'I think I'm past all that. It was only a comparison. Anyway, he doesn't have your *mind* – or Derek's either. But he is devastating to behold, and his singing voice is as goose-bumpy as Johnny Mathis.'

'If that's your idea of goose-bumpy.'

'It may not be yours, but if he goes down half as well in Brighton as he did in Sitges, women will be fainting at the table.'

'Not only women,' Andrew said dryly. 'Did you ascertain which side of the street he plies?'

'You know how timid I am in that area.'

'Hopeless rather than timid. And when is this paragon of beauty and velvety tonsils, sexual persuasion unknown, due to grace the gracious suburbs of Bexhill?'

'I gave him the money for his fare, but all I've had so far is one phone call to say he can't get away yet. Don't say it: there's no fool like an old fool.'

'I wasn't going to say anything,' Andrew said. His tone was gentle. 'I hate to see you let down – again.'

'Do you want to go up to your room now?' Laurence made a point of changing the subject.

'Are we dressing for dinner?'

'I think we might, for your first night.'

'I'll slip into my little black number then.'

'Andrew, you know I hate camp.'

'Sorry, dear – oops, sorry again.'

SARAH WAITED WITH Pilgrim while he filled in forms at the hospital. The registrar directed them to the ward, where one of the nurses reported on Malcolm's condition. Her patient nodded an accompaniment and treated Sarah to beaming smiles. She smiled back sheepishly, uncomfortable with the mute grinning stranger on the over-starched hospital linen.

'Let's get back to the car,' Pilgrim said after only a few minutes. 'See ya tomorrow, kiddo,' he said to Malcolm, who acknowledged the farewell with another nod and beamed at Sarah.

'Has your friend always been dumb?' she asked Pilgrim when they were back in the Bentley.

'I've never heard him speak.' Over his shoulder Pilgrim inspected the capacious rear seat. 'D'you think your dad's ever had it off in this car?'

'Had what off?'

'You know – had sex.'

'I've never heard that expression for it.' She giggled. 'How divine. It's difficult to imagine one's parents "having it off" in *bed* …' she giggled again, 'let alone in the back seat of a car. Anyway, they were divorced before he bought the Bentley.'

'How come you don't live with your mother?'

'She moves around a lot and I was at school in Kent, so it was easier if I stayed mostly with Laurence. I see her every year.'

'Are you still at school?'

She put her foot down and jumped a traffic light as it changed from amber to red. 'No, I don't want to go to university. He's teaching me the hotel business. I help organize wedding receptions and functions at our hotel in Hastings.'

'Your dad hasn't remarried?'

She shook her head. 'Seven years with my mother put him off marriage for good. She's had three more husbands since Laurence and is looking for Number

Five.'

'Does he have a ladyfriend?'

'Not that I know of. She may have put him off women completely. She's a real bitch.'

'What about the housekeeper?'

'She's a bit starchy, but she isn't a bitch.'

'I meant, d'you think they're having it off?'

'My father and Mrs *Danvers*?' Sarah shrieked with laughter. She thought better of jumping another set of lights. The Bentley's tyres growled as she braked heavily.

EVENING

HOPING SHE WOULDN'T be overdressed, Evelyn changed into a calf-length black silk cocktail dress and was relieved to find her host and Andrew downstairs in dinner jackets. Laurence served drinks in a small modern living room with a television which he turned on for the six o'clock news.

Evelyn's worst fears were rapidly confirmed. US naval and air forces were putting the blockade in place. Soviet ships in the Atlantic were steaming towards what was alternately described as a '*confrontation*' and a '*showdown*'. Castro was mobilizing '*hundreds of thousands*' of troops. At UN Headquarters in New York the Russian and Cuban representatives had strongly denied Adlai Stevenson's charges in respect of the missiles. Countermeasures against NATO missiles in Turkey and beleaguered West Berlin were predicted.

Evelyn's tense exhalations of breath provided the only interruption, until Andrew casually observed:

'Perhaps we *had* better go out and get started on

Mrs Danvers' bomb shelter.'

'Don't joke about it,' Evelyn begged.

'Who says I'm joking?'

'We'll have to go back tomorrow,' she said. 'And Sid will *have* to come home.'

'In the unlikely event that missiles do start raining down, I should think we'll be marginally safer here – and Sid in Amsterdam – than in London.'

Her expression was tormented. 'I don't know how you can say something like that and stay calm.'

'I've been very much looking forward to having you and Andrew here this week,' Laurence told her. 'You really mustn't let these wretched politicians spoil your stay. I honestly think this is going to be just a bit of diplomatic sabre-rattling.'

He rose and turned off the television. 'Let me freshen your g-and-t, Mrs Hunter.'

'I'm all right, thank you, Mr Dickinson.'

'I think first names are in order,' Andrew told them. 'Now that we're swigging gin together in the face of Armageddon.'

Laurence gave a grim smile. Evelyn shivered.

THE DINING-ROOM boasted a timbered ceiling, wrought-iron chandeliers, an inglenook fireplace and two heavy oak refectory tables flanked by leather-cushioned pews and throne-like chairs. It was possible to seat twenty people at the two tables. Laurence occasionally hosted dinner parties for local dignitaries and businessmen. He soon began to wish that the other fifteen places were occupied tonight.

Everyone ate too little too quickly – except Pilgrim who ate too much too quickly. Andrew kept the conversation going with reports on London shows and society gossip. Sarah, wearing a long pale-yellow frock, was her usual vivacious self, but Evelyn, in black silk in the pew next to Andrew, contributed almost as little to the conversation as Pilgrim, the brooding leather-jacketed presence in the opposite pew beside Sarah.

When the housekeeper came in with coffee, Andrew was in the middle of a story which allowed him to namedrop Princess Margaret, Cecil Beaton and Greta Garbo.

Laurence mentally compared today's Andrew to the Andrew of 1959, returning to Bexhill after six unproductive months at university and two grim years of National Service, a hardened version of the gauche eighteen-year-old Laurence had briefly met before he went off to college. At eighteen Andrew had been an overgrown schoolboy: knowledgeable and quick-witted, but rudderless – 'all those brains and not an idea in his head,' Laurence's mother would have said. At twenty-one (to Laurence's forty-two) the quick wit had a crueller edge and there was a furtiveness probably developed in response to the trials of the barrack room. He didn't know what he wanted from life, only what he *didn't*: to follow either of the careers his father expected of him. He was insecure and malleable, and it was lucky for Andrew that the hands he fell into were Laurence's. Laurence offered the younger man a refuge from his martinet father, encouraged him to develop a career in display and design, opened his mind to the possibilities beyond Bexhill – and then watched the fledgling flex his wings and fly off into a broader sky.

Now, three years later, the wide mouth with its prominent lower lip, a mouth Laurence had first seen and cherished in the Navy, had acquired a supercilious, almost sneering curl. The dark hair was too long for Laurence's taste; no doubt it was a fashionable length. But the brooding thickly-browed eyes under the flopping hairline hinted at disenchantment as much as derision, disillusion as well as disdain. At twenty-four Andrew combined, it seemed to Laurence, the face of a Chatterton with the air of a Noël Coward hero.

The student had far outstripped his mentor. Andrew today, urbane, sophisticated, made him feel like a country bumpkin. He hadn't seen a musical since *West Side Story*. Lionel Bart and Shirley Bassey were merely names to him, Maggie Smith and Joan Baez not even that. Rising to his feet, he offered port and liqueurs and crossed to a medieval sideboard on which stood decanters and bottles.

'Talking of uppity princesses,' Andrew said, 'when did you last see your mother, Sarah?'

'Last year. She came to London after she divorced Number Four. I stayed with her in Claridge's.'

'Sounds as if her alimony is supporting a better standard of living each time. Number Four was American, wasn't he? Remind me what he did. He wasn't another perfume purveyor like Prince Emilio?'

'No, he's something big in banking.'

'I lose track,' Andrew said.

Laurence laughed. 'So do I, and I was in there somewhere.'

'Is one of your mother's ex-husbands really a prince?' Evelyn asked. Laurence noticed that whenever she addressed Sarah across the table she avoided looking at Pilgrim, who monitored the conversation expressionlessly.

Laurence was still evaluating Evelyn. He had told Sarah that she was not Andrew's mistress, but he didn't know this for a fact. She would be somewhere in her thirties, almost twice the age of the brittle Chelsea blonde Andrew had brought to Bexhill last year whose conversation was limited to the social and cultural activities of the West End and SW3. Mrs Hunter, with her hazel eyes, rounded cheeks and strong jaw, was more like the women of Bexhill than those of Sloane Square; had she originated in the shires? She was small with, he supposed (his ex-wife had exhausted his sexual interest in women), a good bust and good legs.

Her reddish-brown hair had been expertly waved and, he guessed, tinted. She wore little make-up over a lighter tan than Andrew's. Her only jewellery was a necklace of fine pearls and a platinum wedding ring.

'*Was* a prince,' Sarah replied to Evelyn's question. 'This one died before she could divorce him.'

'It was only a title from the Pope,' Andrew elaborated. 'Like getting a peerage from Macmillan for services to the carpet trade and a few fat donations to Conservative Party funds. Presumably the Holy Father reeks of one of Emilio's heady fragrances.'

Sarah giggled. 'Mother wouldn't thank you for that. She still takes being a Highness very seriously.'

'I've always maintained that even as his widow she forfeited the title when she remarried,' Laurence added. He again registered the brooding presence of Pilgrim beside Sarah. 'Anyway, I think that's enough about Louise. Take this young man to the TV room. You can watch *Z-Cars* or *The Avengers* or whatever's on on Tuesdays.'

Sarah smiled at Pilgrim. 'The "grown-ups" are going to brood over lost loves and failed conquests. Shall we stay and pick up a few tips?'

'I think not,' her father said. 'I'm sure Pilgrim would rather have the television on.'

'I'm sure he'd rather have it off,' Sarah said and burst into a peal of laughter. Her hand shook and she spilled Tia Maria onto the table.

'I fail to see any hilarity in whether the television is on or not,' Laurence said. 'And do be careful with your glass.'

'It's that expression. "*Have it off*".' She gestured towards Pilgrim, spilling more of her liqueur. '*He* told me this afternoon. It has' – she giggled – 'sexual over-tones.'

'Sarah, that's enough.' He glared at Pilgrim. 'My daughter has a penchant for vulgarity which I'll thank you not to encourage. Do you have any daughters?' he asked Evelyn. She shook her head.

'No.'

'I sometimes think a good spanking wouldn't go amiss even at Sarah's age,' Laurence said in what he hoped was a light-hearted tone.

Pilgrim stared down the table at Laurence. 'What she really needs to set her straight,' he announced matter-of-factly, 'is a good shagging.'

There was a stunned silence. Laurence opened his mouth, realized he did not know what to begin to say and shut it again. To his surprise it was Evelyn and not Andrew who spoke, her face scarlet with anger or embarrassment.

'I think we can do without that kind of remark,' she said.

Pilgrim turned his eyes on her across the table. The expression on his scratched face was openly contemptuous. 'A good shag wouldn't do *you* any harm either,' he told her.

Evelyn sank back in her chair as if some force were pressing upon her. Andrew gave an awkward laugh.

'Well now, if you don't mind my saying so – forget it; I never spoke,' he said with another abrasive laugh as Pilgrim seemed on the point of a third pronouncement.

Laurence stood up with a sudden movement that pushed his chair into the hearthrug behind him and sent Mrs Danvers' cat skittering with a squeal of outrage from its place in front of the blazing log fire.

'I'D FORGOTTEN HOW bracing this sea air can get,' Andrew said sardonically. He leaned back in a dark-green Chesterfield armchair. Laurence blew a cloud of cigar smoke across the green leather-topped coffee table between them. His gaze traversed the book-lined oak-panelled walls of the library, his favourite room.

'We had some peace and quiet until you got here,' he said.

'I take full responsibility for introducing chaos and disruption into your ordered household.'

'Well, you weren't to know things would get so out of hand. Was I too heavy-handed, sending Sarah and that foul-mouthed young man off to their rooms?'

Andrew raised his glass in a toast. 'Magnificently Victorian,' he said.

Laurence smiled. 'I'm sorry Evelyn's gone to bed so early. I hope this Cuba business isn't going to get her down.'

'She's just a bit overwrought. The accident didn't help.'

'I shall make alternative arrangements with Mrs Danvers as regards feeding our unexpected guest from tomorrow.'

'Let's hope his little friend recovers quickly and we can speed them on the next leg of their "pilgrimage".'

Laurence nodded, sipping his cognac. 'Talking of "little friends", I've been wondering: is Ruth's David the David you played Jonathan to at Hastings Grammar?'

'Yes, he is.'

'Fancy seeing him after all these years.'

'Fancy,' Andrew echoed. He lit a cigarette.

'I'm being tactless,' Laurence apologized. 'Change the subject. How's that pretty new girlfriend of yours – what's her name? – Jocelyn?'

'You're behind the times. I traded her in for a different model. We met at a party of Jocelyn's in Lower Sloane Street. Fiona.'

'What's this one like?'

'Very similar to the last model. I seem to be one of those gentlemen who prefer blondes.'

'*Young* blondes, as I recall. How old is – Fiona?'

'The same age as Jocelyn – nineteen. You'd better start locking up your daughter when I'm around!'

Laurence smiled grimly. 'Like I did tonight! I've left it too late.'

'Tell me about the – young man from Provence, Who led her *une terrible danse*.' He emphasized the limerick rhyme.

'This was last year when she was staying with Louise in Claridge's. I was in Spain. This Frog was doing research at the British Museum library for a member of the Académie Française. I've forgotten how they met but for three or four weeks her phone calls were full of nothing but "Sharlz", the places she was taking him, the shows they were seeing. He was obviously an improvement on the spotty lads at her tennis club. I suppose it was the first serious fluttering of a teenage heart.'

'I remember mine,' Andrew said with an exaggerated sigh. 'Behind the bike sheds it was.'

'Was this David?'

'This was *pre*-David. I was thirteen.'

'Precocious little bugger, weren't you?'

Andrew smiled. 'So did the Frog really turn into a toad and break her fluttering heart?'

Laurence shook his head. 'That was just me teasing her. She was hurt when he upped and vanished, but she got over it once she was back in school.'

'Nothing else got "damaged"? Pardon me for asking, but *les Français* are famously forward in certain areas.'

'She didn't say anything to give that impression and I didn't like to probe. Even at seventeen I considered she was old enough to decide these things for herself and I trusted her – I still do – not to get into trouble.'

'I take back what I said ten minutes ago. Victorian you're not.' They both laughed. Laurence began, finally, to relax as the tensions of the medical emergency, the atmosphere at dinner and Pilgrim's climactic observations eased under the combined influence of the brandy and this 24-year-old man whose company he savoured above all others'.

EVELYN LAY UNDER the blue bedclothes in the blue bedroom, still wide awake. She fretted about Sidney, about the Superpowers' ships steaming towards their confrontation, about the boy she'd put in hospital and – try as she might not to – about the appalling thing Pilgrim had said to Sarah and then to her.

A new novel had been left by her bedside: *The Pumpkin Eater* by Penelope Mortimer. From the blurb she didn't much like the look of it: the marital trials of a metropolitan mother. There were also some fashion magazines, presumably Sarah's choice. Thumbing through one now, Evelyn stopped at a picture of a magnificent evening dress. In the run-up to Christmas there would be dinners and balls. At her height and with her bust (and hair) could she wear ankle-length turquoise brocade? Would she look like any other Jewish merchant's wife (there were so many Jews in the jewellery trade that Sidney was used to being mistaken for one)? Would she look like mutton dressed as lamb? A woman in need of a good shag!

She surprised herself by giggling, then blushed. She heard a distant muffled laugh that could have been Andrew. Faintly there came also the tinny sound of pop music.

CAROLE KING'S 'It Might As Well Rain Until September', still in the Top Ten in the third week of October, came to an end. Another record plopped onto the turntable. A brief hiss of needle static preceded another Top Ten hit: 'Let's Dance' by Chris Montez.

Sarah sprawled on top of her bed in rumpled pyjamas, flicking through the latest *New Musical Express*. Film and fashion magazines were piled topsy-turvily on the floor beside the bed. She caught her reflection in the dressing-table mirror. She looked like any other teenage blonde in rumpled pyjamas with decent skin and no make-up. She also looked cross.

She *was* cross. More than merely cross, she was mightily indignant that Laurence had sent her to bed like an ill-behaved child. And beyond mere indignation, she was monumentally bored. Bored with her father's hotels and her mother's ex-husbands, bored with Ruth and tennis-club boys and moribund Bexhill. Wasn't there more to life than wedding-party lists, tennis, the Playhouse Cinema, *Route 66* and Cliff sodding Richard?

That creepy man was probably right about what she needed. She thought of 'Sharlz', as dark, as handsome (and about as tall) as *Route 66*'s greasily gorgeous George Maharis. She remembered vividly the feel of his lips against her mouth, his hand on her breasts, his thing pulsing in her hand, her heart pounding in her chest.

'*Non, ma chérie,*' she could hear him say as she urged him to go further, to take her all the way; 'ze first time is very important. You 'ave to save yourself for ze right man.' He not only looked like the hero of a soppy magazine story, he spoke like one too.

'Sharlz, nobody's going to be more right than you,' she'd said – another line from romantic fiction. And his teeth had gleamed in his darkly tanned face as he said, '*Ce n'est pas moi, ma chérie*, but you will know 'im when 'e comes.' Just her luck to meet the only French-man with a respect for a teenage virginity!

But the kissing and caressing had been divine. Only one other girl in her dormitory claimed to have touched a man's thing. Then, as abruptly as he'd entered her life, 'Sharlz' had vanished and Sarah was left with her mother, Louise, always maudlin between marriages, offering such Confucian gems as 'That's men for you – can't live with 'em, can't live without 'em.' In one summer Sarah came within a whisker of carnal knowledge *and* matricide.

NO LIGHT SHOWED beneath Evelyn's door as Andrew made his way, unsteady after several cognacs, to the top of the house. From behind Sarah's door Neil Sedaka was reminding her that 'Breaking Up Is Hard To Do'.

Three years ago Andrew had created a filmset-like bedroom for himself in the attic: tented muslin ceiling, walls and bed draped with exotic Liberty fabrics, inlaid Egyptian dressing-table, a camel stool. Intended to evoke a Sultan's palace, really it looked more like a Beirut brothel; the only film that could be set in it would be a *Carry-On*. Laurence's dinner guests, councillors' wives and the like, often asked to see round the house. They were not shown this room, Andrew knew.

As he hung his dinner jacket in a wardrobe concealed behind a swathe of fabric, he recalled Pilgrim's observations at the dinner table. Unchecked, Pilgrim would doubtless have included Andrew and Laurence in the list of those in need of a redemptive shagging. The one Andrew had had last night, which he'd been wickedly describing to Evelyn just before the accident, had not left him feeling redeemed.

Unbuttoning his shirt, his thoughts inevitably turned to the doctor's son, now himself a doctor – 'the David you played Jonathan to at Hastings Grammar'. David, forever fourteen in Andrew's memories of him, now had a wife, a child, another child due any day. Did he sometimes think of Andrew and what they had done together – on the Downs and in each other's bedrooms – ten years ago? What they did had been 'innocent' enough compared to what Andrew had done since then with many others, not one of whom – male or female – had meant a fraction as much to him.

THE GERIATRIC WARD was as quiet as it could get. Some patients snored or talked or made gibbering noises in their sleep. When the night-shift sister sent Ruth to make tea she sneaked down to the medical ward. The duty nurse was alone and dozing at her desk. Ruth tiptoed to Malcolm's bed; he seemed to be sleeping. Then, as she bent over him his eyes opened and his uneven teeth gleamed in the near-darkness. 'Are you all right?' she whispered.

He nodded, still smiling.

'Are they taking good care of you?' Another nod, and then his hands snaked from under the bedclothes, seized her head and pulled her mouth onto his. Startled, she resisted for a moment before surrendering to his probing tongue. *Wait till I tell Sarah*, she thought with glee.

IT WAS ALMOST midnight. Laurence, in cotton pyjamas, turned off the light and crossed to the window to open the curtains. Most nights he would stand there for a few minutes before going to bed, listening to the sea while he reviewed the day's events. Tonight he drew breath harshly.

The surf was audible only as a whisper. Eight miles offshore the foghorn of the *Royal Sovereign* lightship echoed hollowly, mournfully. Tendrils of greyish mist climbed over the cliff and crept along the edge of the lawn.

Against this dark and clammy backdrop the brightly lit uncurtained window over the garage was like another lighthouse beacon in the night. Pilgrim was leaning back in a chair with his large feet resting on the windowsill. His pale naked body was visible to anyone watching from the upper floors of the main house. He was masturbating.

It was the second naked male body Laurence had seen in the last five weeks – also the second in the last two years. At the end of an evening of heavy drinking on the balcony of Laurence's hotel room in Sitges last month Carlo had casually stripped and thrown himself onto one of the beds, passing out almost at once. After a few moments of contemplating the sprawled body, Laurence had drawn a sheet over the young Italian and then fallen onto his own bed half undressed.

In his mind he could still see the slim bronzed muscular body, the tapering 'T' of gleaming black chest hair, the pale flopping penis in its black bush. He compared this vision with the sight of Pilgrim, his skin white and – apart from pale gingery pubes – hairless, the body thick and unsculpted. His penis too was unusually large and thick – not that Laurence considered himself an expert on the subject of penises.

Also in Sitges he had seen, in an art and folklore shop, some vulgar ceramic statuettes: male and female figures with grotesquely exaggerated breasts and genitals. Presumably these homunculus-like sculptures were fertility symbols from primitive or pagan times. Laurence thought of them now as Pilgrim's hand continued to move, slowly, methodically, almost indifferently. His gaze seemed to focus on the unlighted window at which Laurence invisibly stood.

Laurence shuddered in the chill air. He drew his curtains.

IN THE WHITE HOUSE at this time – minutes before seven p.m. – the President was composing a letter to Chairman Khrushchev urging him to respect the quarantine. The US had no wish, he wrote, to fire on any ships of the Soviet Union. He went on:

> *'I am concerned that we both show prudence and do nothing to make the situation more difficult to control than it is.'*

WEDNESDAY

*'... there is always the risk of her mis-
judging and going too far for recall if she
meets no resistance.'*

**THE TIMES, 24 October 1962,
editorial on Russia's spreading
of Communist doctrine and influence**

MORNING

ANDREW LOOKED UP from the *Daily Mirror*. 'It's good to know that even in these critical days the press is maintaining an interest in burning issues. There's an article here on whether next year's Wimbledon tennis queens should be allowed to wear frilly and coloured panties.' He laughed.

'I may as well give up hope of hearing a serious word from you on the real news,' Evelyn said. She shuffled the pages of *The Times* together and folded it neatly. Andrew put his paper down and reached for the marmalade.

'Eat some toast, darling. Let's not face the four-minute warning on an empty stomach.'

'Don't say things like that,' she pleaded.

'Just remember what a great American philosopher once said – or rather, sang: "Que Serà Serà".'

Evelyn was in no mood for jokes. 'What do you suggest we do while this crisis is going on? Go down on the beach and bury our heads in the sand?' She gestured through the glass wall of the conservatory. Beyond the cliff the sun was struggling through a light mist over the sea.

'I'm afraid it's mostly shingle down there, darling.'

Evelyn, pouring herself coffee, briefly contemplated throwing the pot at him. If he called her 'darling' one more time …

'What I suggest we do,' he went on, 'is go all rustic and touristy, inspect a few of the local beauty spots. But we have to start by going to the police station to report yesterday's little mishap.'

'Any news of that boy?'

'Laurence rang the hospital. He's perfectly normal. No more blackouts. They want to run some tests on him, just to be on the safe side.'

Evelyn forced herself to butter a slice of toast. 'Are we the only ones having breakfast?'

'Laurence has gone to Hastings. He has hotels to run. Sarah breakfasted with him, and our Apostle of Shagging is being fed in the kitchen.'

Evelyn blushed. 'Don't remind me of what he said.'

'Sorry, darling.'

ON THEIR WAY out of the house they encountered Sarah in the entrance hall, dressed in jeans and a floppy white sweater. She wore no make-up. A plastic grip with a butterfly ornament held her hair in a ponytail.

'We're off for some sightseeing,' Andrew said. 'Want to come along – if you can stand the company of us judgmental middle-aged types?'

She smiled and shook her head. 'Laurence's garage is salvaging Pilgrim's motorbike. I'll take him to check up on that, then find something to do.'

'Tell your father I'll settle up with him if the bike can be repaired,' Evelyn said.

'Don't worry about that. But make sure you drive safely today!'

'You be careful too,' Andrew said. 'Out with the big bad wolf.'

Opening the front door, Sarah laughed. 'Oh, I think he's all bark and no bite, isn't he?'

Evelyn smiled grimly as she preceded Andrew down the steps. Outside the garage Pilgrim stood waiting in jeans and a clean but unironed white tee shirt, the leather jacket slung over one shoulder. His facial scratches had dried to thin lines. His left hand was still bandaged. Evelyn avoided looking at him as she fumbled with the keys to her Renault.

'I'M SORRY, MR DICKINSON, but neither of the surveyors has come in yet.'

'Okay, Frances. Keep trying, will you.' Laurence replaced the receiver with a sigh. Why was nobody in? Had the crisis over Cuba brought even Hastings to a standstill?

Fighting tiredness, he rose and crossed to the large window which gave a view of the seafront. The A259 was busy as always but the promenade and the beach were almost deserted; the sea was calm beneath the slowly evaporating mist. Laurence yawned.

The image of Pilgrim at the window over the garage returned to his mind: the pale thick body in the bright light so nonchalantly engaged in a public demonstration of that most private of sexual acts. Imagine if Mrs Danvers had seen him from one of her rooms on the garage side of the house! Sarah's rooms were at the other end, facing the road, but Evelyn had a view of the garage from her room next to Laurence's, as did Andrew in his ridiculous attic boudoir. Yet Laurence sensed that he had been the only viewer, unseen but *known* and perhaps even intended. Was he just tired or over-imaginative, or had there been some *malevolence* at work? Gazing out of his office window Laurence shuddered, as he'd shuddered last night at the view from his bedroom.

'LEFT HERE, DARLING,' Andrew said as the De La Warr Pavilion came into sight, dominating the seafront. On the journey down from London yesterday he'd told her that this Art Deco landmark was the 'magnet' that drew many visitors to Bexhill, an otherwise unremarkable, stuffy resort. Evelyn had mixed feelings about Art Deco. Sidney had taken her to Barcelona some years ago, where she was enchanted by the extravagantly fluid lines of the city's Art Nouveau buildings. Art Deco architecture was more formal, more austere, although

Evelyn cherished an Art Deco brooch Sidney's craftsmen had made for her, copied from one commissioned
from Asprey's by Edward VIII for Wallis Simpson
before he abdicated and made her a duchess.

Andrew noticed her glance at the De La Warr. 'It'd
be a shame to lose that,' he said. 'Let's hope the
Russians don't drop one of their missiles on it.'

'Or anywhere else,' Evelyn said soberly.

THE MOTORCYCLE WOULD be ready tomorrow; the
garage had ordered a new exhaust. Sarah offered to
take Pilgrim for a spin in her Morris Minor.

'D'you think Andrew and Mrs Hunter are "having it
off"?' she asked as the road wound through Pevensey.
Pilgrim glanced incuriously at the castle ruins.

'What, right after breakfast?' he said with a laugh.
Sarah sniggered. 'Anyway,' Pilgrim went on, 'he's a
turd-burglar, isn't he?'

'A what?'

'You know – a queer.'

'What makes you say that?' Deciphering his collo-
quialism, she winced.

'Well, he looks like one and talks like one.'

'He's a bit affected, but I don't think he's queer. My
father's met some of his girlfriends.' She overtook the
car in front, earning an irate honk from an oncoming
van driver.

'Where does that woman come into the picture?'

'Andrew has a business with a chap he worked with
in Selfridges, doing shop window displays and posters
and programmes. Mrs Hunter's husband is their
backer. He's in the diamond business.'

'I thought only nancy-boys did window dressing.'

'No, there are some normal ones, apparently. So,
does Mrs Hunter strike you as a happily married
woman?'

'Perhaps her old man doesn't give her what she

needs and she's hoping to get it from Andrew.'

'Yes, but *is* she?'

Pilgrim began to roll a cigarette, deftly, using only his unbandaged right hand. 'No,' he said. 'You can tell when a woman's getting what she needs, and she hasn't got that look.'

AFTER THE FORMALITIES at the police station Andrew navigated the eighteen miles from Bexhill to Bodiam, at Evelyn's insistence using only main roads. As they walked towards the castle in watery sunshine he gave her a resumé of what he remembered of its history from childhood visits. She listened passively and followed him over the moat and through the gatehouse into the ruined interior where they encountered a group of schoolgirls in the care of a harassed teacher. Andrew led Evelyn up the narrow winding stairs of the southwest tower to admire the vista of river and woodland and hop-fields.

'Do you think Sarah's all right?' she asked at the top.

'They're probably still at the garage.'

Evelyn put her hands on the parapet and then, finding the stone clammy to the touch, thrust them into the pockets of her fur coat. 'What if they're not? She shouldn't be out with a foul-mouthed beatnik like him. He might – you know – *try* something.'

Andrew laughed. 'Darling, here we are in the area conquered by the first Normans and you're worrying if Sarah's drawers are being invaded!'

Evelyn blushed. 'She's not much older than those girls down there. I think we should at least have warned her father.'

'What can Laurence do? Lock her in a chastity belt? This isn't 1066. If Sarah wants to lose her virtue to a foul-mouthed beatnik, assuming she hasn't already lost it to some spotty local oik, I'm inclined to say Good Luck to all who sail in her.'

She stared at him in amazement. 'You're unbeliev-
able. Suppose it *is* her first time. Don't you know how
important the first man in a girl's life is?'

His expression mocked her. 'You think Sarah
needs to lose her cherry to someone like your Tony?'

Evelyn paled. Inside the fur coat her body seemed
to slump. 'How do you know about Tony?' she asked in
a faltering voice.

'Sorry, darling. It's not very fair of me to drop it on
you like that. Sid let slip about your long-lost RAF lover
in the pub after work one night. I had the impression
he's still very jealous of him.'

'My God,' Evelyn said. She took several deep
breaths before she could speak again: 'For your information, Tony wasn't the first man in my life – not in the
sense we're talking about.'

'Why, Evelyn, don't tell me your past is even more
salacious than your husband led me to believe.'

Her lip trembled. 'Don't make fun of me, Andrew.
Not about this.'

The sound of young voices echoed in the doorway
behind them. They waited for a break in the schoolgirl
chain to descend the stairs and return to the car-park.
Inside the car she began to cry silently, the tears pouring down her face.

'My dearest,' Andrew said. He held her while she
wept against his chest for several minutes. Part of her
registered the fact that after three years progressing
from handshakes to brotherly pecks on the cheek, she
was now, finally, being held in his arms. When she
straightened up and blew her nose and dried her face
with a tissue, he lit two cigarettes and handed her one.
Evelyn drew on it deeply: the taste of menthol always
reminded her of chewing-gum. Avoiding his concerned
and questioning expression, she stared unseeingly at
the view outside the windscreen.

'Sid was – the first,' she said finally. 'Not Tony. Tony wouldn't. Not till we were married, he said.'

'Did he win medals for gallantry? According to my mother even Bexhill and Hastings became Sodom and Gomorrah for the duration.'

'Even our little village in Devon,' Evelyn said, her voice gaining in strength. 'Three drunken engineers from Tony's airbase attacked me one night. He saved me, driving past in his jeep. That's how we met. Did Sid tell you that part?'

'No: only that you were engaged to this Tony during the war.'

She watched two dogs chase each other across the grass. 'We weren't really engaged. He said it wasn't fair to get engaged or married in wartime. I think he knew he was going to die.'

'Oh. Well, Sidney obviously thought you and Tony were lovers.'

'We weren't. Our honeymoon was my first time.' She blushed. 'I thought he knew that.'

'Sid's been jealous of a – *ghost* – for no reason all these years.'

'I ought to have told him. But we've never talked about – that side of things – just as we've never discussed why I haven't got pregnant since my miscarriage in our first year.'

'You should see a specialist, both of you if necessary.'

'We've left it a bit late to start a family,' she said tonelessly. 'Sid turns fifty next year.' Winding down the window, she dropped her cigarette onto the ground. 'So ...' she faced him with a forced smile, 'now you know. There wasn't anyone before Sid and there's never been anyone since. Well ...' she hesitated, 'not really. I nearly had an affair once, when I was staying in a hotel in Torquay while Sid was on one of these Dutch trips. The man was German, very charming, very correct, a little bit forward. Anyway, I didn't. Perhaps if he hadn't been German ...' She gave a short laugh. 'Almost an adulteress. Not going all the way with Tony. Nearly raped by those soldiers. It's the story of my life: *nearly* this, *almost* that. I've probably *not quite* been a good wife to Sid. Still, I don't suppose he'd complain.' She gave another harsh laugh. 'We've been *almost* happy.'

Andrew stroked her left hand on the wheel. 'My poor darling,' he said.

BY THE TIME they reached Newhaven Pilgrim was hungry. Sarah parked beside a fishing pier and smoked a cigarette while he ate fish-and-chips from a newspaper. 'How many women have you had it off with?' she asked impetuously.

'Jesus.' He laughed with his mouth full. 'How often have I had fish-and-chips – or a shit?'

'Is that all it is to you? Like eating or going to the lavatory?'

'It's nothing to make a song and dance about. Being a virgin, you wouldn't know that.'

Sarah went red with anger and embarrassment. 'Whatever gave you that idea?'

'You are though, aren't you?'

'That's for me to know and for you to find out,' she said with forced bravado.

'Maybe I will,' he said, still chewing, 'and maybe I won't.'

AFTERNOON

ANDREW AND EVELYN explored Rye's quaint cobbled streets on foot before lunching in the oak-beamed dining room of the Mermaid Inn. Evelyn declined to join him in the game pâté and only picked at a sole meunière while Andrew devastated a large lobster.

'What *he* said last night,' she asked, stirring a cup of coffee as he launched into his second crêpe suzette, 'do you think it *is* the answer?'

'Darling' – he grinned – 'you're a married woman and I'm a bachelor. *I* should be asking *you*.'

Evelyn released her spoon. 'I've already told you,' she said seriously, 'my experience has been very limited. Sid and I haven't exactly – set the Thames on fire.' She managed a wan smile.

'You must have had your moments – even if the earth didn't always move.'

Evelyn's colour rose. She leaned forward and spoke softly not to be overheard by their neighbours. 'What you asked me yesterday, about – faking with Sid. I don't really know what it is you're supposed to fake.'

Abandoning the crêpe, Andrew wiped his mouth on the napkin. 'Are you telling me you've never – well, never had an orgasm?'

She stared at the tablecloth. 'I'd never heard that word before I met you. And until you gave me *Lady Chatterley* to read I still didn't know what it was.'

He laughed. 'Penguin Books may have a lot to answer for!' Evelyn's head remained lowered. He stirred sugar into his coffee before continuing:

'I'm sorry if I've given you the impression it's such a big deal. Fiona's not the first girl I've caught faking an orgasm, and Jocelyn *was* the first one who seemed to have one every time.'

She sat back and looked at him. 'All these girls you've been – seeing, did you *love* any of them?'

'"*Leuv*"? What ees zees sing called "*leuv*"?' he said, parodying the voice of Maurice Chevalier.

'Be serious, can't you. Have you honestly never loved anyone?'

'I might ask if *you* have ever loved *dis*honestly, Mrs Hunter.' Now, eyebrows raised, he was Noël Coward. Evelyn banged her cup down.

'I thought we were having a proper conversation for once. Or is that beyond you?'

He looked – or affected to look – contrite. 'Sorry, darling,' he said in his own voice, that 'darling' as irritating to Evelyn as his impersonations. 'Yes, I have honestly been in love, but not with any of these girls I've been "seeing".' He raised his eyebrows again to provide inverted commas mocking her euphemism.

'But wouldn't you like to settle down with some-body?' The thought entered her head that she envied him a little: no ties, no commitments. It didn't enter her head that he might envy her.

'Of course I would,' he replied, 'but Fiona's not that somebody. I enjoy having her in my bed, but I don't want to share my life with her.'

He drank some coffee, then smiled. 'There, one of my secrets for two of yours. I still owe you one!'

Evelyn forced a smile in return. In the three years she had known him – morning coffee encounters in Fortnum & Mason's, after-work drinks in Piccadilly or Park Lane, restaurant dinners and theatre evenings with or without Algie and Sidney, a dozen dinner parties given by the Hunters and perhaps half-a-dozen cocktail parties at Andrew's flat (he didn't give dinner parties, professing no aptitude in the kitchen) – in three years she had never discussed her marital life with him. And yet today she had told him her most intimate secrets: why?

'All this confessional stuff,' Andrew added: 'is it because Kennedy may be about to start World War Three, or because of what Pilgrim prescribed last night?'

Evelyn tried not to blush. She leaned forward again. 'It's nothing to do with him – or with President Kennedy,' she said bitterly. 'It's all *your* fault. Even before I met you I knew there was something missing, but at least I didn't know what it was. It's all so bloody unfair.' Leaning back, she caught her cup with her elbow, knocking it over the side of the table onto the floor.

'IS SARAH THERE with Ruth, David?'

'No, she isn't. Ruth's not up yet. She did a night shift last night.'

'Where can the wretched girl be? She's not at home either. I suppose she's out with that bloody loud-mouth.'

'Is that anybody I know?'

'The chap who came with the boy you took to hospital.'

'Oh, bit of a loudmouth, is he?'

'The thing is, the hospital's phoned to say they're ready to discharge the boy. My housekeeper doesn't drive, Andrew's out with his ladyfriend, I'm due at a staff meeting and now Sarah's disappeared.'

'*I* can go and collect him if you like. I'm not doing anything. Obviously he's all right?'

'They said he should take it easy for a couple more days. He'll have to stay with us. Are you sure you don't mind picking him up? I'm very grateful.'

'Not at all. And I'll look in on him tomorrow on my

way to the yacht club.'

IN BRIGHTON SARAH parked the Morris and they went on the Palace Pier. Pilgrim won a rubber duck in the shooting gallery which they took down to the beach and used as a target for stone throwing.

He beat her at Crazy Golf. Then they went on the Dodgems. Sarah screamed with excitement; Pilgrim drove with a view to colliding rather than dodging and on their second go they were cautioned by the attendant. He won a handful of coins on a roll-a-penny slide and led her into a seedy café on the lower promenade where Sarah's high spirits and her appetite evaporated. With an observation about 'good food going to waste', he shovelled a pile of greasy sausage and chips from her plate to his.

'What else is there to do?' he asked as the waitress took Sarah's ten-shilling note to the till.

'Shouldn't we get back for when they let your friend out of hospital?'

'No hurry for that. Let's go to the pictures.' He'd counted out eight pennies to tip the waitress. Sarah thought wryly how gratified her tennis club friends would be if they could see her now, here. To hell with them.

'That James Bond film might be on,' Pilgrim said.

AFTER LUNCH ANDREW directed Evelyn a few miles beyond Rye to Camber Sands. Evelyn's city shoes were ill-suited to walking on the soft terrain. They sat in the Renault and watched as the tide turned, the waves encroaching fast on the broad sandy beach.

He told her how he and his sister had come to this beach as children with their parents, sometimes also with the wife and children of a local bank clerk, now the bank's manager, to whom Andrew's mother had once been engaged. 'This was after the war,' he said.

'During the war Camber was fenced off and mined because it might have given the Nazis an easy invasion route.'

Evelyn didn't want to talk about the war. The war meant Tony and all that his death had cheated her of.

'Do you suppose Sarah played on this beach when she was little?' she asked, distantly concerned about what might be happening to Sarah if she was still with the horrible motorcyclist and at the same time relieved not to be talking about herself, the failure she had made of her life.

'I'm sure she did,' Andrew said. 'She was born in '44. Once the mines and barbed wire were cleared, Laurence and Louise would have brought her here. There isn't this much sand on the beaches in Hastings or Bexhill.'

'How long were they married?'

'Seven years, I think.'

'What was she like – Louise?'

'Well, she may sound like Hastings' answer to Barbara Hutton, but at heart she's still the barmaid he married during the war.'

'I thought Laurence was just a friend from your hometown. I didn't realize you'd lived in his house and done some of his decorating.'

'This is going to make us evens in the secret-swapping department,' he teased her, aware as he did so that behind this 'secret' lay the *lie* that he had lived to the Hunters and most of his London friends for the last three years, and to his family for much longer. Evelyn smiled. He said:

'I met Laurence in 1956, just before I went to university. My father was the contractor when Laurence added a new wing to his hotel in Hastings to cope with the rising demand for seaside holidays. And in 1959, a few weeks after I came home from National Service, I moved in with him in Cooden. Louise had been gone since 1950. She went off with an East End clothing tycoon who brought his mistress to Hastings for a dirty weekend and swapped her for Louise. Not that Laurence took the mistress in part-exchange, I should add!'

'He's never remarried?'

'No, I think he prefers fathering to being a husband – even with a precocious brat like Sarah.'

'Was she with him when you were living under his roof?'

'No, that summer she went on a cruise with Louise and the perfume prince.'

'Why did you move in with him?'

Andrew thought how easy it would be to answer with the truth: *I was the lover Laurence had lost but never really had, a bit like you and your Tony*. He answered with a partial version of the truth:

'I had to get away from my father. We were rowing all the time. My mother couldn't cope with it, and it was hard on Sylvia, my sister. While I was off doing my National Service Dad revived his old dream of me joining him in the building trade, like he'd joined his father. But I didn't even want to *teach*, which was what I'd said I would do when I went to university. He couldn't accept my becoming a window dresser.'

'Well, I can see his point of view as well as yours,' Evelyn said. 'As a parent you'd expect more of a boy who was bright enough to get to college.'

He shrugged. 'But look where it's got me. I did languages at university, but my favourite subject at school was Art, and I think I always knew I'd do something in the commercial art field. Window dressing was just a place to start.'

She turned on the ignition. They took the A259 back to Winchelsea whose harbour, like its grander neighbour Rye's, had silted up and turned to marsh in the 16th and 17th centuries. After inspecting two of the medieval town gates and the parish church they went into a self-consciously 'quaint' tea-shoppe.

'Why have we waited three years to have our first serious conversation?' Evelyn ventured.

He raised his eyebrows. 'Because I'm not really a serious person?'

'I think you are. Underneath.'

'Oh dear. I'm not going to ask "Underneath what?"'

'You understand me better now. I'd like to understand you too.'

He shook his head. 'There's not much to understand.'

'There is, but you hide it all the time.'

He gestured through the leaded window. 'I'm like the marshes out there: a stagnant swamp where once the tides came in and out and ships from many ports sailed.'

'You're too young to be talking about stagnation.'

'In the circles in which I used to move you start to worry about ageing before you reach twenty-five.' He came out with this without thinking what a revealing reply it was – though not perhaps to Evelyn.

'Which circles are those?'

He averted the moment of danger – of revelation – with a wagging finger. 'Enough of your probing. Our travelling Dr Kinsey has got a lot to answer for. He and his little chum must be halfway to France by now.'

WHEN THE TARANTULA crawled up James Bond's body Pilgrim scared Sarah with a tickle on her neck; he wolf-whistled at Ursula Andress's scantily clad appearance. Sarah hated the film, hated James Bond, hated her uncouth companion. How much preferable were the boys she dated from Good Families in Bexhill: 'snogging' in the back row of the Playhouse Cinema; doing the Twist at tennis club parties; swigging absent parents' sherry and gin; necking in the car; sometimes going a bit further – but never 'all the way'. And yet the virginity Pilgrim had unerringly identified was, especially since 'Sharlz', increasingly irksome.

A gale of laughter swept through the audience at some new antic on the screen. He nudged her with his elbow. 'Great, isn't it?'

'Isn't it,' she echoed. Sarcasm was wasted on Pilgrim.

Yes, she was impatient to be relieved of the burden of chastity, but – *today* – by this greasy slob with peasant tastes and the manners of a pig?

Absolutely not.

LEAVING WINCHELSEA, THEY continued on the A259 towards Hastings, turning off at Fairlight, where Andrew pointed out two houses his father had built and a cliff-top street where erosion had toppled some of the homes into the sea. Parked near the coastguard station, they dozed for an hour amid gorse-covered hills rolling down to low cliffs.

PILGRIM INSISTED ON staying for the next showing of the supporting film. A dozen or so people also stayed on, and another hundred came in for the late afternoon show. The B-feature was a crass story about a wealthy American woman with twin daughters, one as elaborately goody-goody as the other was evil. The audience hissed and booed both sisters and treated some scenes to slow handclaps and foot stomping. After half-an-hour Sarah could stand it no longer.

'Come on,' she said. 'Let's go. This is tripe.'

'It's good for a laugh. What's the big rush?'

'Your friend must be wondering where on earth you've got to.'

RETURNING TO THE music room with a large pink gin and a glass of Mrs Danvers' homemade lemonade,

Laurence found Malcolm inspecting the framed photographs on top of the grand piano. The boy smiled at him. He pointed to a black-and-white picture of an eighteen-years-younger Laurence, slimmer, short-haired, in naval uniform, with a woman whose hair was richly waved and a baby swaddled in a crocheted blanket.

'Yes, that's Sarah,' Laurence said and then, as Malcolm tapped the glass over the untypically maternal-looking Louise: 'and that's her mother. We were divorced when Sarah was six. My ex-wife has had three more husbands since then. No,' he found himself volunteering, 'I've never remarried. Once was enough for me.'

The boy smiled. He picked up a colour photo of Laurence with Andrew. Andrew's hair was shorter, Laurence's was fuller and less grey, but otherwise they looked much as they did today. 'That was 1959,' he told Malcolm. 'Andrew lived with me for a few months' – (he could have said exactly how many months, weeks, days, it had been) – 'until his work took him to London where he lives now.' It was surprisingly easy to talk to the silent smiling boy.

Malcolm picked up another black-and-white picture that was three years older than the christening photo: Laurence, with a beard, stood on board a warship beside a younger man, also bearded; both wore naval uniform. Laurence swallowed.

'That was 1941,' he said. 'My father served in the Navy during World War One, and I did the same when the Second War started.'

The boy tapped the glass over the younger man.

'His name was Derek,' Laurence said. 'I was the First Lieutenant and he was Second Officer. The ship was a corvette, an escort ship for the Atlantic supply convoys.'

He swallowed again. 'About a month after that

picture was taken, one of the freighters in our convoy was torpedoed and we went in to get the men off before she sank. The deck was ablaze, they couldn't launch any boats, so we went in closer and threw a climbing-net over the side and the men jumped for it. Some of them were terribly burnt and screaming. Derek and I were with the rest of the crew hauling them over the gunwale as they came up the net. One man slipped and hung by his broken leg halfway down the net and Derek went down to help him and then the freighter suddenly listed towards us and maybe a wave pushed them or us as well and the two ships came together with a clang which I still sometimes hear in my sleep.'

Aware that he was almost gabbling, he broke off. Malcolm was no longer smiling. His expression was curiously blank, as though he lacked the repertoire of appropriate responses to a story such as this. Laurence swallowed noisily again before continuing:

'It happened so suddenly they didn't have time to scream or – anything. And when the two ships came apart again there was nothing there but some blood on the ropes which the next wave washed clean.' This was not true, but Laurence had never been able to bring himself to describe what he had briefly glimpsed before the sea swallowed it up, something which, with the noise of the hulls colliding, still haunted his dreams.

'He was like the brother I never had,' he found himself gabbling on. 'And when Andrew came into my life it was as if I'd found him again. They're very alike. If Derek didn't have the beard you'd see it in their photos. Only because I was seventeen years older and Andrew was the same age as Derek had been, he was more like the son I never had. That's why we're still very close, even though he doesn't live under my roof any more – apart from the odd visit, like this week.'

He managed to stop himself from confessing to this

boy who was no older than Sarah that he hadn't had a sexual relationship with Derek but wished, desperately sometimes, that he had; whereas he had, three years ago, had a sexual relationship with Andrew and rather wished that he hadn't.

He smiled, a little sheepishly, at Malcolm who found a gesture with which to respond. He put down the photograph of the two sailors, took Laurence's left hand in his right and held it against his own cheek, down which a single tear ran.

EVENING

THERE WAS AN *Evening Argus* on the banquette beside Evelyn abandoned by a customer or supplied by the landlord. She read the front page while Andrew was buying drinks. Under the headline '**ZERO HOUR FOR U.S.**' it reported Russian ships '*steaming onwards*' towards the blockade. Another story, headlined '**BERLIN – REDS ARE MOVING**', reported '*massive military convoys*' on the move in East Germany.

'Still think I'm overreacting?' she said, thrusting the newspaper at him when he returned with gin for himself and sherry for her.

He glanced through the two stories, then picked up his glass. 'Well, drink up, darling. It's a bit early to eat again, but at least we can drink and be merry, if you really think that tomorrow we die.' He toasted her and drank.

Evelyn left her sherry untouched. 'I just don't know how you can be so cavalier about it.'

He put his glass down. 'We used to debate World War Three in the Sixth Form and at university. Most of my contemporaries seem to think a nuclear holocaust in our lifetime is pretty well inevitable. *I've* always thought that only a madman would start one.'

Evelyn stood up. 'I shan't feel happy till I talk to Sid,' she said. 'Have they got a phone box here?'

'If not, there's one outside. You'll need a lot of change to call Holland.'

'I'll reverse the charges.'

The pub had no telephone, so she went to the box opposite the general store-cum-post-office, glad of her fur coat in the dank early-evening air of the South Downs outside Hastings. The local operator put her through to Continental, where a woman with a strong French accent demanded three shillings and four-pence as a deposit on a personal transfer-charge call which she then confiscated by making Evelyn press Button 'A' before telling her that Mr 'Unter was unavailable. Evelyn returned to Andrew.

'He's not in. I suppose he's dining out.'

'Did you try the Red Light District?' he teased. The unlikely prospect of her husband with the Amsterdam prostitutes in their notorious windows overlooking the canal brought a smile to her lips. She picked up her sherry glass.

'So, is a pub crawl your idea of drinking and merry-making?' she asked him, a little surprised to find that she too could be sanguine in the face of annihilation.

SARAH TOOK THE A27 on the return journey, which was more direct and would bring this excursion to a speedier conclusion. Dusk was deepening. Back on the A259 outside Pevensey the engine began to overheat. The headlights illuminated a muddy opening to a farm gate; she pulled into it and switched off the engine.

'Now what?' asked Pilgrim. His only attempt at conversation since they left the cinema had been to request another meal, which Sarah curtly told him he would either get at the hospital or back at the house.

'We wait,' she answered his question. 'This car doesn't like long journeys. I've got some water in the back – and a torch. When it's cooled down a bit I'll top up the radiator and we can go on.'

'I'm starving.'

'We'll be in Bexhill in ten minutes.'

'And I need to piss.'

'Well, you can't do it here.' A car went past in each direction.

'Yes I can,' he said and got out of the car, leaving the door open. Over the faint soughing sounds of the marsh she heard Pilgrim urinating through the gate, disconcertingly loud, like the pissing of an animal. He must have a thing the size of a horse, she supposed and almost giggled aloud.

Another car passed; its lights illuminated his leather-jacketed figure at the gate and, beyond him, the swathes of mist rising from the dykes to create an eerie chequerboard over the marshes.

He got back into the car, closing the door. There were rustling noises as presumably – she didn't look – he finished readjusting his clothing.

'Come on, then,' he said.

'You have to let it come off the boil before you take the cap off.'

He laughed and said: 'The car's not the only thing that's coming to the boil.' Seizing her right hand he pulled it over to his lap. She glanced down as another car passed, casting a glow over what she could now feel against her knuckles. His trousers were open, exposing his rock-hard penis. It was longer and thicker than any other Sarah had ever seen or felt, including Sharlz's which had been bigger than any of the local boys' – and, like Pilgrim's, circumcised. It smelt of fresh urine.

'For God's sake!' she said. 'Are you mad? With all these cars on the road.'

'They can't see through the back of the seats, can they? Go on.'

'Go on, what?' She tried to free her hand but he held it too firmly. He didn't answer her question. Another car passed: in the glow of its headlights Pilgrim's penis was ghostly white and cast a moving shadow onto her lap. Sarah wrapped her hand round it and did not let go when he released her wrist. She stroked it up and down rapidly, clumsily. Where Sharlz's and some other boys' penises had felt smooth and elastic, Pilgrim's felt gnarled and knobbly like a rough-hewn stick. The top of it was damp.

'Not too fast,' he said. The local boys liked a brisker pace. 'That's better.' Sarah lacked the bravado to tell him she was not a complete novice. He made a sort of grunting noise, then said: 'I'll fuck you if you want.'

'Not here you won't,' she replied quickly. *Not here, not anywhere*, she thought: *I'm not going to lose my virginity in the back of a bloody Morris Minor*. But then, as with another animal grunt he ejaculated into her hand – more copiously than the last boy she had masturbated in the car after an evening at the pictures – it occurred to her that the back of this or some other car *was* most likely where, soon enough, she would part with her virginity.

An odour that reminded her of Mrs Danvers' porridge had replaced the smell of urine. Passing him some tissues from the glove compartment and wiping her hand clean she knew with absolute certainty that she would 'go all the way' with the next boy, whoever it was, who asked her to toss him off in the car. A wank, a fuck: what's the difference? Either way you just felt used. At eighteen Sarah was already beginning to feel used up.

She opened her door and got out to deal with the

still steaming radiator.

THE HOUSEKEEPER HAD warmed a bed in the last of the guestrooms, at the front of the house between Sarah's bedroom and the guest bathroom which Evelyn and Malcolm would share. 'Your chauffeur will have to sleep on one of the sofas,' she warned her employer as they took their second refugee upstairs. 'If the Russians don't blow us to smithereens before he gets here.'

'It will certainly resolve our accommodation problem if they do, Mrs D.' He kept a straight face.

'You may mock, Mr Dickinson,' she sniffed, 'but there were some alarming opinions expressed on Cliff Michelmore's programme while you and this lad were eating your dinner.'

'I think the word you want is "alarmist". These professional doomsayers have been predicting the end of the world for so long that I refuse to give them any credence. The Russians didn't declare war over the Bay of Pigs last year, and I don't believe they will now.' He was about to remind her of the Soviet blockade of Berlin in 1948–49, but Malcolm had started undressing to change into one of Sarah's less garish pyjama suits and Laurence felt suddenly embarrassed in front of the housekeeper. 'I'll leave you to it,' he said and left the room. Mrs Danvers had been an auxiliary nurse at a military hospital during the war and was used to undressing patients.

Returning to the bedroom a few minutes later, he found Malcolm alone and already asleep, snuggled under the bedclothes with only his head showing. Laurence felt an urge to cuddle up beside him, just for the mutual comfort, not with a view to any kind of molestation. He settled for ruffling the tousled black hair. Malcolm murmured a rumble of contentment, reminding Laurence of a snoozing puppy.

As he returned to the landing he heard a car – two cars – pull up outside, one of them Sarah's distinctively rattling Morris Minor.

'OH GOD,' EVELYN said as she parked on the opposite side to the garage, 'he's still here.'

'Don't worry, darling. I shan't let him open his mouth.' He smiled as Sarah approached the Renault, Pilgrim hanging back beside Sarah's Morris.

'Have you had a nice day?' she enquired in her hotel hostess tone.

'Very stimulating, thank you.' Andrew replied. 'How was yours?' Sarah laughed grimly.

'Stimulating just about describes it,' she said.

WHILE ANDREW AND Evelyn were dozing at Camber and Sarah and Pilgrim were watching *Dr. No* in Brighton, the first 'showdown' of the Cuban crisis had taken place.

A twenty-vessel Russian 'armada' approached to within a few miles of the American blockade which already consisted of twenty-five destroyers, plus cruisers and carriers, support ships and submarines. Sonar showed a Soviet submarine submerged between the two ships leading the convoy. US Defense Secretary Robert McNamara ordered the aircraft carrier *Essex* to depth-charge the submarine if it ignored signals to surface.

At 10.25 a.m. Washington time it was reported that some of the Russian flotilla had stopped dead in the water. Six ships stopped, then twenty. An oil tanker, the *Bucharest*, ran the gauntlet and was allowed to proceed on to Havana without being boarded. Other tankers and an East German passenger ship continued to steam towards the blockade. But fourteen ships turned back.

In letters to President Kennedy and Chairman

Khrushchev that day and in a statement to the United Nations Security Council, Secretary-General U Thant reiterated a pledge that:

> *'I shall gladly make myself available to all parties for whatever services I may be able to perform.'*

THURSDAY

'… to sink or not to sink …'

**DAILY SKETCH, 25 October 1962,
on the decision facing the Commander-
in-Chief of the US Atlantic Fleet**

MORNING

ANDREW SMILED AS Evelyn entered the conservatory. 'Don't look so glum, darling. The world has made it through to one more dawn.' With an effort Evelyn produced a thin smile.

'You're as bad as Sid. I got through to him first thing this morning. They don't get the London papers till lunchtime. He asked me who won the war.'

'Bravo, Sidney. He's not planning to rush home, then?'

She reluctantly sat down on the opposite side of the rattan cane table. 'He's rushing to buy several times what he intended,' she said. 'People with cash to spare always move into gold and diamonds when there's talk of war.'

'Well, I must come up with another day of diversions while we wait for the next showdown at the barricades.'

Evelyn poured herself a cup of coffee. 'We've got to stay in this morning. I saw Laurence when I got up to call Sid and he's asked us to keep an eye on Malcolm till lunchtime. Sarah's gone into work with her father, and Mrs – Danvers – is going into Bexhill on the bus to help the cook with the shopping.'

'What about our other unmentionable guest?'

'He's been told to steer clear of us and keep himself amused. Oh, and the doctor's going to look in on our patient.'

'Shall we ask him to give you something for your nerves?'

'I don't need – oh, why do I fall for your teasing

every time?' She threatened to throw a slice of toast at him. Andrew raised his hands in surrender.

'YOU'VE NOT GOT much to say for yourself this morning,' Laurence said as he pulled into his parking space in the hotel forecourt.

'That's right, I haven't,' Sarah replied.

'Is anything wrong?'

She shook her head.

'Not worrying about this Cuba business, are you?'

She shrugged. 'Most people my age expect the world's going to be blown up sooner or later. We don't lose any sleep over it.'

'Oh dear,' Laurence said, stunned by this matter-of-fact announcement. 'Would you like to get away for a bit? You could go and stay with your mother. She'd be glad of your company while she's between husbands.'

Sarah made a face. 'No thanks! Bexhill and Hastings may be boring, but anything's better than visiting Mother.'

'Even me?'

'Even you.'

'Is it really so boring around here?'

'Yes,' she said.

Was this the restlessness of youth, he wondered, or a legacy from Louise? He sighed. 'You would tell me if there was something wrong, wouldn't you?'

She shrugged again. 'I might.'

'Well, that's not much of an answer.' He started to open his door, then turned his head back to her. 'You didn't have any – trouble – with that chap yesterday? I wish you hadn't spent the whole day with him.'

She met his eyes. 'He didn't try and give me the shagging he said I needed, if that's what you're worried about.'

'Sarah! For God's sake!' This was the Modern Child speaking, not her mother. Louise had been common but, like many a wartime barmaid, almost prim in her speech: less so now, since living in America. He frowned at her, this fine-boned blonde who was the image of his own mother but so often sounded like nobody he knew. Unusually communicative today, she went on:

'Not that it's any business of yours, but – nobody has so far. So I don't know whether he's right or not about it being, you know – what I need.'

Laurence took her hand and felt instantly uncomfortable. Having started this conversation, which he wished he hadn't, he couldn't leave it here. 'I know we don't usually talk about this sort of thing, but – don't be in too much of a hurry. In my day we weren't so impatient to try everything. Even your mother, although she wasn't what you'd call a blushing virgin on our wedding night, which I' – he blushed now himself – 'almost was, she wasn't at all the marital rattlesnake she became after we parted.'

'I've never begun to understand why you married each other in the first place.' Sarah too was uncomfortable with this intimate dialogue.

'Oh well, that's easy. Louise married me because I was one of the first men – and certainly the most promising – to offer her a proposal rather than a proposition. And from my point of view, it was all because there was a war on. I – I'd seen men die. I assumed I would die too before it finished, and I wanted to experience marriage before I died. Selfish of me, I know, but then I would have left her a lot better off as a widow than as a barmaid in your grandfather's hotel. I also wanted a child. And I got you.' He patted her hand, redoubling Sarah's discomfort.

Then he released it and reached again for the door handle. 'We've got work to do. We'll just do a half-day, so as to get back to our guests, but you've got a wedding reception and a Rotary dinner to catch up on.'

He had actually enjoyed their unusually close conversation and wanting to end it on a light note, he added: 'Of course the wedding I'm really looking forward to is *yours*!'

'Fuck off, Dad,' Sarah said, also speaking from the heart.

'Sarah! Really, you go too far.'

'I'VE TOLD HIM he can get up as long as he doesn't do anything too strenuous,' David Yates announced, joining Andrew and Evelyn in the conservatory, where they were on their third pot of coffee. 'I've never actually met a mute before. It's weird.'

'If you think he's weird, you should meet his friend,' Andrew said.

'A bit of a loudmouth, Mr Dickinson said.'

'Loudness is just the start of it.'

'Where *is* he, by the way? I want to impress on him that this boy won't be up to any motorcycling for another day or two.'

'He's gone into town to see if his bike's mended.'

'Do they really have to stay two more days?' Evelyn asked.

'Well, I don't think the boy is ready for Continental travel, if that's what they're planning.' He abandoned his coffee. 'I'm off to the yacht club. Fancy a spot of sailing, Andy?'

Andrew smiled. The abbreviation of his name belonged, like David, to another era. 'I don't think so, *Dave*,' he said with deliberate emphasis. 'I haven't done any since we left Hastings Grammar. And Florence Nightingale needs me here.'

'Oh no,' Evelyn said, 'I can look after the boy till the others get back. You go and have a sail, Andrew.'

'You'll need to change,' David said.

'Into what?' Andrew arched his eyebrows.

'You can't come sailing in white trousers and a

blazer.'

'Ideal for a yacht, I'd have thought.'

'It's not that sort of yacht, as you perfectly well know. Haven't you got some jeans and an old sweater?'

'No, I haven't,' Andrew retorted. 'I can steal a sweater from Laurence, but I am not getting into a pair of his baggy trousers.'

'Oh well, I've got spare clothes in the car, to come home in. You can have the jeans, though I'm probably a couple of inches bigger than you in the waist. And it means once I get wet, I'll have to stay wet and risk getting a cold.'

Perhaps it was because he'd followed his father into Medicine, but this slightly garrulous fusspot was not the David Andrew remembered.

AFTER THEY LEFT, Evelyn took the coffee tray to the kitchen where she discovered Malcolm – in the white tee shirt and jeans in which he'd been thrown off the motorbike, newly washed and ironed by the house-keeper – peering into the refrigerator. He grinned impishly.

'Are you hungry?' she asked.

He nodded.

'I'll make you a sandwich. Or would you rather have bacon-and-egg?'

He nodded. The doctor was right: it was weird.

'You're not helping. Bacon-and-egg?'

He nodded.

'Or sandwich?'

He shook his head.

Evelyn explored the large unfamiliar kitchen, which had a walk-in larder like an old-fashioned pantry and an Aga stove. The boy sat at the worn pine table as she remastered the art of cooking on a range. Soon he was eating while Evelyn made a fresh pot of coffee.

Sitting down opposite him, she took her cue from the room they were in as a way of breaking her own silence.

'We had a stove like that in my parents' kitchen in Devon. Do you know Devon?'

Malcolm shook his head.

'Well, that's where I grew up,' she soldiered on. 'My husband too, though he's from Okehampton, which was the nearest big town to our village. I met him just after the war when I went from working in the local post office to the bigger one in Okehampton. He was work-ing in his father's shop a few doors away. His father was a watchmaker. After we got married we moved to Exeter. He went to work in the jewellery department of a big department store and I transferred to another branch of the GPO. Then my husband was offered a job in Selfridges in London – do you know Selfridges?'

Malcolm shook his head again.

'Anyway' – Evelyn was getting into her stride now, although it occurred to her that her life story might be of limited interest – 'that's how I met Andrew. Not straight away, but my husband was friends with the head of the display department who became Andrew's boss when Andrew went to work there three years ago. My husband had left by then. An uncle of his who'd emigrated to Canada died and left us some Canadian Pacific Railway bonds and we used that money to lease a shop of our own, a jeweller's of course. But we stayed friends with Algie and he introduced us to Andrew. They have their own business now, they're graphic designers.' She almost told him that Algie was homosexual, but it wouldn't do to gossip.

Having somehow progressed with what seemed to be brilliant logic from Okehampton to Bexhill by way of Oxford Street, she concluded: 'So that's how I come to be here with Andrew while my husband's in Holland buying diamonds.' In fact, she realized, her being in

Bexhill with Andrew was hardly a logical consequence and could easily be misconstrued, but perhaps this was enough for now. At least she'd managed not to mention Tony or the German in Torquay. 'More coffee?'

Malcolm, who had smiled throughout, nodded and held out his cup.

From the road came the sound of an approaching over-revved motorcycle. Evelyn's hand, holding the percolator, trembled. The sound continued past the house and receded into the distance. She steadied her hand and poured.

DESPITE LIVING IN suburban outer London David had kept up his sailing on lakes and reservoirs and coastal holidays. Andrew had not and, after six years, expected to have lost the knack but it quickly came back; he hauled and let go, leaned and ducked in response to David's instructions and felt once more the exhilaration of a billowing sail and the water's hiss beneath the hull as they tacked out into the Channel on a light breeze under a clouded sky. A flood of memories also returned of his teenage years, dominated, on the debit side, by a father whom it had been hard not to hate and, on the plus side, by this one classmate whom it had been disconcertingly easy to love.

When they came within sight of the lightship and its surrounding submerged sandbanks, David took down the sail and they wallowed and drifted in the barely discernible swell while he produced a thermos of coffee and doorstep sandwiches.

'This takes me back,' Andrew said, ignoring the instinct to keep his nostalgia to himself.

'Me too,' said David. His broad easy grin and breeze-tousled hair tormented Andrew, who could have reconstructed from memory every muscle and sinew beneath the other's lifejacket and cableknit sweater. He risked going further.

'Don't you sometimes long for those days?'

David's expression became serious. 'I suppose so. After a particularly bad day in the clinic or' – another grin – 'don't quote me – when my mother-in-law comes to stay. "We didn't do it like this in my day",' he mimicked. 'Maybe then I wish I was sixteen again, with nothing more to worry about than the next maths exam. But then I look at my son and Mary and our life and I find it impossible not to count my present blessings.'

Andrew could think of no reply to this that would not sound bitter or cynical. He moved onto safer ground by asking: 'Where did you meet your wife?'

'At medical school. She's had to give up work while we get going on a family, but she helps me with some of my research.'

'What are you doing research in?'

'Venereal diseases.' He laughed without embarrassment. 'I'm not a GP like my Dad. I work in a VD clinic in Croydon. Syphilis is my speciality.'

'I'm always hoping it won't be mine,' Andrew said.

'I beg your pardon? Ah,' he laughed again: 'I get you.' A wave rocked the boat and they braced their backs against the gunwale. 'You're not married yet, are you?' David now asked, unwittingly steering the conversation back into dangerous depths. Andrew shook his head.

'If I'd married young like you did, I think I'd have at least one divorce under my belt, like Laurence.'

'Sarah's told Ruth you had a girlfriend here last year. Is Mrs Hunter her replacement?'

'No, she isn't.'

'I hope you don't mind us talking about you behind your back.'

'It's better than *not* being talked about,' Andrew couldn't resist saying. David's response was a surprise:

'Oscar Wilde!' Another grin on the first face Andrew had ever kissed. 'But – if you don't mind me asking – are you happy with this carefree and glamorous life-style?'

'Is it glamorous?' Andrew retorted. He resisted adding a sardonic reference to Croydon. 'No, I don't mind you asking. I'm afraid *happiness* is a club whose membership I seem to be blackballed from.'

'For the life of me I can't see why.' David's expression registered genuine concern. Andrew longed to take him in his arms. He also longed to shake him out of his cosy domesticated complacency. He threw caution overboard:

'D'you remember what we used to do out here on the ocean wave when we were about half the age we are now?' David again surprised him by laughing rather than going scarlet.

'Weren't we daring! Of course, you know, lots of boys that age do that sort of – stuff. It doesn't mean anything.'

Andrew winced. 'But how many boys swear un-dying love for each other?'

Now David blushed. 'Oh dear, did we? I've forgotten that part of it.'

I remember every detail of all of it, Andrew could have said. There was more he could have said, ached to say. Settling for a borrowed epigram, he said, more casually than he felt: 'I still cherish what the poet called "*les neiges d'antan*".' David screwed up his face.

'That's not fair. You were still doing French when I switched to Biology.'

'It's Paul Verlaine. "The snows of yesteryear".'

'Andy, you always were more of a romantic than me,' David said. He threw the dregs of his coffee over the side and set about raising the sail. Andrew was still thinking of the things he yearned to say. Unsure of his own intentions, he suddenly stood up and made to move to David's side of the boat. Whatever his intentions, nothing came of them. A gust of wind filled the rising sail and the boom swung before David could tension the rope. Andrew's eyes filled with tears as the boom cracked him across the shins. Then he fell into the sea.

AFTERNOON

LAURENCE TELEPHONED THE garage to check on the motorcycle, only to be told that a young man in a leather jacket had collected it mid-morning. But there was no sign of Pilgrim when he and Sarah returned home for a late lunch in the conservatory with Evelyn and Andrew and Malcolm.

The boy's silent presence generated little of the unease that had hung over Tuesday's dinner. His appetite was as hearty as Pilgrim's but he attacked his food with less blatant greed. He smiled at anyone who looked at him.

After the dessert Sarah announced: 'I'm off to Ruth's for a game of tennis before it gets dark.'

'Take Malcolm with you,' her father said.

'He mustn't play tennis,' Evelyn interjected. 'The doctor said he's to take it easy for two more days.'

Malcolm smiled at her.

'He can watch anyway,' said Laurence. He dispensed coffee as Sarah and Malcolm departed. 'There's not much left of the afternoon,' he added, 'and it looks like we're in for a shower. But shall we go for a drive anyway – have tea somewhere?' He looked at Andrew, but it was Evelyn who answered:

'I'd rather stay in if you don't mind. I don't want to miss the six o'clock news.' Although she made a point of not looking at Andrew, it was he who spoke next:

'Can't we forget Cuba for an hour or two?'

'Maybe *you* can, but *I* can't.'

Laurence intervened. 'I'm sure you're right to be concerned,' he told Evelyn. 'Anyway, there's plenty of time before the news. Instead of going out, I shall show you round my flowerbeds. Andrew, you needn't come. We know you're not the horticultural type.'

'I expect Dorothy Parker had people like me in mind when she said, "You can lead a horticulture but you can't make her think".'

Laurence forced himself to laugh at a quotation he deemed inappropriate in front of Evelyn, on whom it was apparently wasted; she said nothing.

'I shall go down on the beach,' Andrew went on. 'Recapture a few more memories of my misspent youth.'

Laurence gestured out the window. 'Be careful on the stairs down to the beach. They're a bit rickety. Having survived drowning this morning, I don't want you breaking your neck this afternoon.'

'I shall trip down them as light as a fairy,' Andrew assured him and was rewarded with a reproving frown.

'HE KISSED ME in the hospital on Monday night,' Ruth bragged, gesturing at Malcolm who sat, smiling, beside David Yates and his extremely pregnant wife on a bench overlooking the tennis court. 'He put his tongue in my mouth and everything.'

'Did he really?' Sarah hesitated before divulging her own small secret. 'That friend of his got his you-know-what out in my car last night.'

'*Sarah*! He didn't!'

'He *did*,' Sarah said emphatically and with some smugness.

'Whatever did you do?'

'What I always do.' She affected nonchalance. 'I – you know –' Nonchalance deserted her, and she reddened as she made an up-and-down gesture with one hand.

'Oh my God. Did – stuff – come out?'

'Of course it did. Doesn't it always?'

'Yuck.' Ruth made a face. The probationary nurse, used to coping with male blanket-baths and bedpans, was squeamish at the thought of ejaculation.

'Come on, you two,' David shouted from the side-lines. 'Are you here to tittle-tattle or to play tennis?'

TOO WARM IN the heated greenhouse, Evelyn loosened her fur coat. 'I know you and Andrew think I'm being ridiculous ...' She tailed off.

'I wouldn't want you to think I'm as flippant about these things as Andrew,' he said, deadheading a purplish spiky-flowered chrysanthemum. 'You're not alone in feeling that we're on the brink of a precipice. Mrs Danvers feels much as you do, and so does my secretary in Hastings. Sarah told me her generation fully expects mine to blow the world up sooner or later.'

'Andrew said his classmates all felt the same. He's the odd man out.'

'Well, I'm still inclined to think the storm is going to blow out before it causes any damage,' Laurence said, but Evelyn was not looking for reassurance.

'It's the worst thing that's happened since the war,' she said. Then she found herself blurting: 'I lost the man I loved in the war. That's not to say I don't love my husband, but I did sort of – settle for him on the rebound.' Now her smile was one of acute embarrassment. 'I don't know why I'm telling you this. I feel as if I'm coming apart at the seams. Lots of people lost someone in the war. I expect you did too.'

'Yes,' he said. 'I lost somebody I loved very much.'

A few raindrops pattered onto the greenhouse roof.

'Did you marry your wife – on the rebound as well?'

'I suppose I did.'

'Maybe that's why it ended in divorce. Oh, excuse me, I'm being very presumptuous.'

He smiled. 'No, no, it's an interesting theory, though I think there's quite a bit more to it than just that. Anyway, yours seems to have worked out – even if your husband was your second choice.'

'Oh well, we had financial struggles in our early years, and I lost our baby ... Those are the sort of things that cement a marriage together, however shaky its foundations may have been.' The rain became a steady drizzle, streaking the glass above them.

'I suppose Sarah provided the only "cement" in my marriage and as you may have gathered, she means more to me than she does to my ex-wife.'

'I hope you know how lucky you are,' she said. 'If I'd only had a child, maybe I'd be able to take things like this Cuba business in my stride.'

He shook his head. 'No. You'd have more to lose.'

'It doesn't seem to work that way with you.'

'It doesn't, does it!' He laughed. 'Maybe I'm just more of an optimist. And talking of which, here comes the eternal Pollyanna.'

Evelyn smiled at this analogy as, beyond the weather-beaten gazebo at the eastern end of the clifftop garden, Andrew appeared at the top of the rickety wooden stairs from the beach. He'd turned up the collar of his jacket and looked pale with cold.

Laurence laughed again. 'I'm afraid his walk down memory lane has given him another brush with pneumonia.'

EVENING

THE SIX O'CLOCK news on BBC television seemed to endorse Andrew and Laurence's view of the crisis rather than Evelyn's. After a summary of the day's developments over Cuba – a Russian oil tanker had been allowed through the blockade; a dozen ships had turned back; the Queen had referred to the 'dangerous situation' in her speech at the State Opening of Parliament – the presenter hurried on to other, seemingly more important items.

Unemployment had topped 500,000 for the first time since 1959. Alf Ramsey had been announced as the new manager of the England football team. John Steinbeck had won the Nobel Prize for Literature.

'Football before literature,' Andrew said. 'Oh, England, my England!'

Evelyn felt cheated of some cataclysmic development that would vindicate her anxiety. Laurence, less complacent than he would have liked Evelyn or Mrs Danvers to know, sipped his pink gin and made no comment. If Andrew felt like gloating, he managed not to show it.

There were just the three of them at dinner. Sarah had telephoned to say that she and Malcolm were dining with Ruth's family. Pilgrim's absence provided the topic of conversation over soup:

'He may have broken down again,' Laurence suggested. 'I didn't think to give him our phone number.'

'Perhaps he's just scarpered,' said Andrew. 'Gone to France or wherever.'

'What do we do with the other lad if that's the

case?' Evelyn asked.

'Laurence can adopt him!'

Evelyn was not in the mood for humour. 'Be serious, will you. Have you found out anything about him?' she asked her host. 'Where he's from. His family. That sort of thing.'

'No, I haven't. Did you know he's illiterate? I asked him to write down the answers to those sort of questions yesterday, but he can't write. He can't even *draw*. How would he get anywhere on his own?'

'Then I suppose we'd better hope Pilgrim comes back to cope with him,' Andrew said.

'*He* gives me the willies,' Evelyn confessed.

'What, our silver-tongued doctor of psychiatry?' Andrew teased her.

'Filthy-mouthed is more like it. There's something dirty – no, worse than that – something *depraved* – about him.' She turned to Laurence. 'I worried about your Sarah being out with him yesterday.'

Laurence thought about what he had witnessed from his bedroom window on Tuesday night and his feeling about the incident, reviewing it in his office yesterday. Was he becoming infected with the 'Cuban virus' of irrational anxiety?

'Aren't you forgetting his healing hands?' Andrew asked. 'Not what you expect from a "monster of depravity", surely?' His tone continued to mock Evelyn. 'He practically raised Malcolm from the dead.'

Laurence suppressed a shudder. 'You didn't mention this on Tuesday.'

'He's talking rubbish,' Evelyn retorted. 'The boy came to of his own accord. *And* he blacked out again when we got here.'

'Thus guaranteeing we'd have to put a roof over their heads. "*Ensnaring us in a web of terror and deceit*",' he added in the sepulchral tone of a third-rate film trailer. Not for the first time since the unfortunate collision in the wood, Evelyn found herself shivering with apprehension.

After the meal they moved to the music room where Laurence and Evelyn played solo whist while Andrew played snatches of show tunes on the piano.

'If you get tired of graphic art, you can come and work for me,' said Laurence. 'Play in one of my bars.'

'Do a double-act with your dazzling new chauffeur, perhaps?' Laurence shot him a warning look.

Andrew launched into a Chopin Étude, played faultlessly, yet – to Laurence's ear, better attuned than Evelyn's – mechanically. He followed this with Debussy's 'Claire de Lune', adding some rippling arpeggios in the style of Liberace. Evelyn applauded when he finished. Laurence went off to replenish their drinks.

AFTER DROPPING RUTH off at the hospital to begin another night shift, Sarah drove inland. Having run out of small talk to which Malcolm could smile and nod, she concentrated on the road, driving fast and with a grim determination.

Just inside a track leading into a wood – on the other side of which, a few miles away, Evelyn had collided with the motorcycle – she stopped and switched off the engine. They sat in silence and total darkness for a few minutes. The rain clouds had moved northwards, but the chill night air slowly enveloped the car with mist. Malcolm seemed unperturbed by their location and her silence. Suddenly, but not impulsively – Sarah had resolved this course of action during dinner at the Yates's – she leaned over and kissed him fiercely on the mouth.

His lips parted under hers and they tongued each other's mouths. Twisting awkwardly across the gear lever and the gap between their seats, he fondled her small breasts through the sweater she was wearing and then inside it. Reaching down, she opened the zipper of his jeans and manoeuvred his penis out of his underpants. Not as large as Pilgrim's, it was about the same size as others she had held in this car, in this wood, in this dark. She smelt Palmolive soap, which might have been him or his penis. Not knobbly like Pilgrim's, it felt silky, throbbing in her hand; he was uncircumcised.

This was the point she'd reached before, a dozen or so times with a half-dozen boys before Pilgrim. Now she pushed Malcolm onto his seat which she tilted as far back as it would go. Kicking off her plimsolls, she pulled off her jeans and slid down her panties. As she turned round and moved across she almost slipped and surrendered her despised virginity to the gear lever.

Not quite horizontal, Malcolm lay on his back in the dark car, his invisible erection poking through his fly. Grunting as she climbed on top of him, he stretched his hands up under her sweater and forced his fingers inside her bra to stroke her nipples. Braced against the roof she grasped his penis in one hand and then, moist with anticipation, lowered herself onto it.

The virginity from which she was so keen to be parted left her with a flare of pain, a bit like squeezing a pimple. She rode his penis up and down, experimenting with different strokes and timing. She ran the hand with which she'd held him under his tee shirt: beneath the fur-like hair his skin was velvety and warm. He grunted and began to buck his body under her. Sarah thought she would be able to come, though not as easily as when using her fingers, but the chance was missed when Malcolm tensed and then subsided under her, disconcerting her with the closest he'd come to articulate speech:

'Aaah,' he said through parted white teeth, the only part of him that was visible in the clammy darkness of the mist-shrouded car.

ABANDONING THE PIANO, Andrew had moved to a gold-brocade fauteuil with the Penelope Mortimer novel while Laurence and Evelyn continued their game of whist. Shortly after ten Sarah came in to announce that she and Malcolm were back.

'Did you have a nice evening?' Laurence said.

She smiled. 'Very nice, thank you.'

'Is the boy all right?' Evelyn asked.

'He's fine. He's gone to the kitchen. I said I'd fix him a sandwich. Why are boys hungry all the time?'

'Perhaps he's still growing,' Andrew offered. Sarah almost smirked at this.

'Have you and Ruth managed to extract any more information from him?' her father enquired.

'How could we?'

'His friend seems to have vanished off the face of the earth.'

'Isn't he back? The light's on over the garage.'

'*I* put the light on so he could find his way in. His motorbike's not there, is it?'

'No.'

'I'm trying to persuade Laurence to adopt Malcolm,' Andrew said. His raised eyebrows teased her. 'How d'you feel about having a new brother?'

'"No, thank you" is how I feel,' she replied blithely. 'I'd better go and feed him. Cook won't take kindly to him poking around her kitchen. Goodnight, everybody.' She kissed her father's cheek – something she usually only did after some extravagant act of generosity on his part. When Andrew ostentatiously held up his head she kissed him as well and smiled at Evelyn before leaving the room.

Evelyn stood up. 'I think I'll turn in too,' she said. 'All this sea air seems to make me sleepy.'

'Help yourself to the phone if you want to call your husband again,' Laurence said. 'And please don't reverse the charges. I know how much we hoteliers bump up the price of calls.'

'That's very kind of you, but I'm sure he'd prefer me not to keep pestering him.'

When they were alone, Laurence topped up their brandies. Andrew dropped his novel onto a gilded side-table.

'A woman's book, isn't it?' said Laurence. 'I bought it with Evelyn in mind.'

'A bit near the knuckle for her. It's about a woman whose marriage is so arid that she takes refuge in staying more or less continually pregnant.'

'But isn't Evelyn's marriage childless?'

'Yes, hers is sterile physically *and* emotionally.'

'I think you do her an injustice. We had a cosy chat in the greenhouse and she led me to understand that even though she married on the rebound from a chap who died in the war, it's worked out pretty well.'

Andrew raised his eyebrows again. 'A *very* cosy chat, from the sound of it.'

'It's nothing she said, but I get the impression that she's a little bit in love with you. But then' – his expression became rueful – 'aren't we all?'

'Well, there's a thought to bring joy to the heart of an old maid on the shelf,' Andrew said.

Laurence laughed. 'I think the dust rarely gets the chance to settle on your particular shelf,' he said. Andrew grinned and toasted him with the last of his brandy.

Laurence raised his glass. 'Tell me, Andrew, these girls of yours in London – do they make you happy?'

Andrew lit a cigarette before answering:

'David asked me that question on his dad's boat this morning – just before I threw myself overboard.'

'I thought you fell.'

'I'm exaggerating, for dramatic effect. Mind you, a few more seconds and he might have *chucked* me over the side. I think I stood up with the idea of throwing myself on *him*.'

'You don't feel he would have welcomed this fanning of an old flame?'

'He's become something of a stuffed shirt.' Andrew exhaled smoke with a sound like a sigh. 'I believe I was keener to "unstuff" him than try to fan old flames. Old, *cold* flames. By the way, did you know he isn't a GP in Surrey?'

'What does he do, then?' Twisting in his chair, Laurence lifted the brandy decanter from a chiffonier behind him.

'He works in a VD clinic.' Andrew held out his glass.

Laurence grimaced as he poured. 'Perhaps he does that so that he can get to handle lots of – you know – private parts.'

Andrew also pulled a face. 'Suppurating ones! Rather him than me! I suspect that people who specialize in that area of medicine don't get a sexual thrill from their work so much as a warm glow of righteousness!' He laughed.

'So did your immersion prevent you from answering the "happiness" question?' Laurence persisted.

'I fobbed him off with a line stolen from Groucho Marx. Just yesterday I told Evelyn that I sometimes yearn to settle down, improbable as it may sound. Not with any of these current "girls of mine", I should add. If there is a "*Miss Right*" for me, I haven't found her yet. But today's little nautical adventure seems to show that I still yearn to sail in the waters on the other side of the bridge.' He drank some of his brandy. 'And if matrimony is liable to turn me into another version of David, maybe I'd do better to continue steering my present erratic course.'

He looked bleakly at Laurence, who responded with a sympathetic smile.

'I suppose "*No*" is the honest answer to your question,' Andrew went on. 'I'm *not* happy. But I wouldn't say that I'm *un*happy either. Who says we have a God-given right to be happy, anyway? Are *you* happy, Lorenzo?'

Laurence shook his head. 'No, I'm not, but I think I am *contented*. At my time of life one begins to set a great store by contentment.' It was his turn to sigh. 'But I fear you're not even contented.'

'I should be, God knows. Business is good. I enjoy my work. I adore my flat. London's a great city to live in, especially if you've got money. A whole bevy of sex-pot girlfriends.' He stopped to inhale from his cigarette. 'The latest of whom has just started treating me to a few home truths. Mostly in bed.'

'I don't recall having any complaints in that area,' Laurence said with another smile which Andrew reciprocated fondly.

'You were rather less demanding than Fiona. According to her I'm *too* considerate between the sheets, too anxious to please. Women like a man to be more aggressive – Fiona does anyway.'

'Are women ever easy to please – in bed or out of bed? Louise certainly wasn't.'

Andrew lifted his brandy-glass in another toast. 'Absent friends and ex-wives,' he said. 'Long may they remain absent!'

Laurence raised his glass with a laugh. 'Amen to that!'

SARAH, IN BED, felt like hugging herself with excitement. Not a virgin! At last! She'd almost shouted it in the music room. She couldn't wait to tell Ruth.

Then, as she reviewed the experience with Malcolm, her excitement evaporated. There wasn't much to it, was there? Perhaps it got better after the first time, or perhaps there was more you had to do. She knew you could get books on the subject, although surely not in Bexhill.

Ruth didn't know anything; the Russians would probably blow the world up before *she* lost her virginity.

Who else could she ask: Mother? Sarah giggled aloud at the notion of this.

She thought about Pilgrim. Doing it with him would really hurt, wouldn't it? Did you have to work your way up the sizes before you were ready for ones like Pilgrim? Was it easier to – what was the scientific word for 'come off'? – with the big ones? If only she'd done it with 'Sharlz': he could have taught her everything she needed to know.

She began to feel a little tingly down below, where there was also a faint soreness. It was funny, she thought sleepily, but losing your virginity was a beginning rather than an end. There was still so much to learn.

LAURENCE LOOKED IN on Malcolm before going to his own room. As last night the boy was visible only as a tousle-haired lump under the bedclothes. Laurence bent over and touched the side of his face lightly. Malcolm went 'Hmmm' without waking.

Perhaps I should have remarried, Laurence thought, the thought, twelve-and-a-half years after Louise, taking him by surprise: *I could have had more children.* It was ironical that Andrew had made a joke on this very point.

A son, he thought. *If only I'd had a son.*

He sighed a deep sigh and tiptoed out.

ANDREW SAT UP in bed, smoking a last cigarette and sipping the last of his brandy. The 'Happiness' question with which he'd been bombarded today continued to nag at him.

What Fiona and Jocelyn and two similar girls who'd preceded them in the last two and a half years contributed to his life was an ornamental audience at restaurants, shows and parties and, as Pilgrim might baldly put it, 'something to shag'. Happiness was not involved; neither was Love.

He thought about the years, only a handful of them, before he made what Algernon Farley called his 'crossing to the other side of the bridge'. On the side he had left, Love was sought by some, often desperately, but it always seemed a sickly, possessive sort of love. Between a platonic friendship with Laurence when Andrew was eighteen and leaving school and their uneasy six-month sexual liaison when Andrew was twenty-one and leaving home, there'd been university and National Service. Bristol University he remembered chiefly for a tortured relationship with a neurotic fellow student which, if he was honest, had contributed more to his decision to drop out after two terms than disenchantment with his studies. Gareth's father was chairman of a steel works and of a Welsh rugby team. Scared to death of being found out or, worse, arrested and bringing disgrace to his family, Gareth was reluctant to push the sexual boat beyond schoolboyish mutual masturbation; this, which had seemed daring and tender to Andrew when he'd done it with David at Hastings Grammar, was no longer enough: he was eager to try more, try everything.

National Service was where he first entered the shadowy world of men who lived two lives: the uncouth camaraderie of the barracks and the furtive fraternity of off-duty encounters in parks and public toilets. Sexual frontiers were approached and briefly crossed, but of necessity everything had to be hurried; there was little satisfaction beyond release and relief.

He'd hoped that Laurence would 'mentor' his final graduation into the realm of fully adult sex in 1959, but Laurence had even less experience than himself and was almost as inhibited as Gareth. It was Andrew who took the initiative in their bedroom activities (Laurence

was the first person since Gareth with whom he had
sex on a bed), making the older man feel like the
reluctant 'pupil'. Laurence, far more than Andrew, was
always conscious of the twenty-year gap in their ages
and the fearful consequences they faced if caught or
betrayed. Scandals had engulfed John Gielgud in 1953
and Lord Montagu of Beaulieu in 1954; in the eyes of
the law Laurence's infatuation with Andrew was as
unnatural and criminal as Oscar Wilde's with Alfred
Douglas. Andrew was one of those for whom the risk of
falling foul of the police gave sex an added frisson;
perhaps less so now, with a business and a reputation
to lose.

Looking back tonight, Andrew had to peer across
almost a decade to pinpoint a time when he had been
truly happy. Before and beyond Fiona and Jocelyn,
Laurence, Bielefeld and Catterick Camp and Bristol
there was only *David*: True Love rendered innocent by
ineptitude and made doubly tender by the shabbiness
of all that had happened since.

He sighed, drained the brandy glass, stubbed out
his cigarette and turned off the light.

EVELYN COULDN'T SLEEP. Her mind whirled with the
huge mess Kennedy was getting the world into and the
smaller mess she'd made of her life. She went
downstairs in her dressing gown to phone Holland. If
she just spoke to Sid – solid, sensible Sid – he would
put her mind at rest and she'd be able to sleep. When
Andrew poured scorn on her anxieties, he only served
to aggravate them. When Sid – and perhaps, today,
Laurence too – made light of them, they did become,
for a while at least, a little lighter.

It was after eleven, the central heating was off, the
house felt chilly. There was a short wait for the local
operator and a longer wait for the Continental Exchange. The hotel operator answered within seconds

but then there was another long wait, total silence on the line, before he came back and announced that there was no reply from Mr Hunter's room. 'Any message?' he asked.

'Do you wish to leave a message, Bexhill?' the Continental Exchange operator amplified.

'No,' Evelyn said. Where could he be, at this hour – after midnight in Holland?

'Do you wish to defer the call?'

'No, thank you. I'll book again in the morning.'

'I shall have to charge you the personal fee if you cancel.'

'That's all right,' she said. She hung up. Surely he wouldn't sleep through the phone ringing next to his bed? Perhaps he'd gone out for dinner with one of his suppliers. There was one who always invited Sid to his home for a meal.

As she closed the study door behind her she noticed a light in the kitchen at the end of the corridor off the entrance hall. Was Malcolm on the scrounge again? He might need help with another sandwich. She went down the passageway and opened the kitchen door.

A figure was bent over peering into the fridge, but it wasn't Malcolm, it was Pilgrim, dressed in a terrycloth robe that was too small for him, tight in the armpits and short in the sleeves. He looked up and grinned. 'Hello,' he said amiably. 'Did you think I was a burglar?'

Evelyn felt oddly relieved to see him and too angry at his daylong absence to be intimidated by his appearance, barefoot, in Mrs Danvers' kitchen. 'Where've you been?' she demanded. 'We thought you'd gone off and left Malcolm.'

'He's okay, isn't he?'

'That's not the point. We've all been worried. Where have you been?'

'I took the bike for a run and ended up in London.'

'*London*! Whereabouts in London?'

'Walthamstow, if you must know.'

'*Walthamstow*!' Why was she repeating everything he said? 'Is that where you come from?'

'Round there.'

'Do you want me to fix you a sandwich? I suppose you haven't eaten all day.'

'I just came in to get a glass of milk, that's all.'

Managing not to provide another echo, Evelyn went to the cupboard where tumblers were kept and took one out. A milk bottle in one hand, Pilgrim closed the refrigerator door with the other. As he turned to take the glass from her his robe, held by a loose sash at the waist, fell open, exposing his naked pale body and his large flopping penis. His pubic hair was gingery blond.

'Cover yourself up, for God's sake,' Evelyn said, her anger overcoming any sense of outrage or threat.

'Aren't you enjoying the view?' he asked, coming nearer. Evelyn took a step back.

'Don't be ridiculous,' she said, still angry.

'I bet you don't see many of these.' His tone was insolent rather than aggressive. He took another step towards her and relieved her of the tumbler. Evelyn took two steps back and pulled her dressing gown tighter, as if protecting her modesty in the face of his lack of it.

'For God's sake,' she said again.

'I bet that queer hasn't got anything like this.'

'What queer?' she asked and immediately thought of Algie, who was the only homosexual she knew.

'Andrew.'

'He's not – like that. He's had lots of girlfriends.' Why was she trying to defend Andrew to this insolent stranger in an undersized bathrobe whose oversized organ – Evelyn started to tremble – was rising in her direction?

'So I've heard, but I reckon I know a queer when I

see one.' His penis surged to full erection, sticking out of the open robe like a truncheon, a truncheon that he was bearing inexorably towards her. Evelyn remembered her first impression of him in the woods, kneeling over the unconscious Malcolm, holding the boy's skull as if he intended to crush it. Well, now *she* was to be the Wild Man's victim, and this time his intent seemed to be rape rather than murder. She backed into the corner beside the door to the pantry.

'Don't come any closer,' she said. Her voice quavered. There was nothing on the gleaming white counter beside her to defend herself with. She contemplated darting into the pantry where she might be able to barricade herself inside or at least pelt him with tins, but he was already too close for escape. 'I'll scream,' she warned him.

'I don't think so,' he said. 'This is what you've wanted since Tuesday. This is what you *need*.'

Evelyn started to say 'Don't be ridiculous' again, but she was now trembling too much to speak. Pilgrim set the glass and the milk bottle on the counter, came one step nearer and placed his hands on her shoulders. Evelyn looked frantically around her, looked anywhere but down where she could feel his rigid organ prodding into her robe.

Now his hands pushed down on her shoulders until her knees buckled. Naïvely she wondered why he was forcing her to her knees if he intended to rape her. The pressure on her shoulders continued until she was kneeling on the linoleum floor. Close up, the club of flesh now pressing against her face looked enormous, loathsome; she closed her eyes but still felt it against her cheek, hard and knobbly with inflated veins, and pulsing. It smelt of bath soap with an underlying odour that was a little like dough, a little like musk.

'You know what to do,' he said harshly.

'No I don't,' she stammered; her husband had

never put her in this position and nothing in any novel she had ever read had prepared her for Pilgrim.

'Open your mouth.'

'Oh God,' Evelyn said as his intention became plain. 'No, don't make me.'

But he did make her. He bent his own knees so that the swollen column brushed her lips. She tried to turn her head away but he yanked it back with one hand and forced her jaws apart with his other hand. Evelyn imagined the door opening and someone – the housekeeper! – finding her in this position: the mortification might be greater than her relief at being rescued. She tried to lean back but he only pressed harder towards her and – it wasn't possible – the suffocating mound of flesh entered her mouth and began to slide to and fro. Her hands flailed at his chest, his thighs. She snorted breath through her nostrils. He pumped harder; she could feel her teeth scraping the turgid column, but he seemed impervious to pain.

'How d'you like that, you stuck-up bitch?' he snarled as he pumped her gaping mouth. Choking and snuffling breath through her nose, Evelyn wondered if it was his intention to stifle her to death. Then he said 'Jeeesus Christ,' his thighs tensed and her throat filled with a viscous fluid: she tasted sour milk mixed with something that wasn't exactly flour and something else that wasn't exactly fish paste. She had no choice but to swallow it. Then, as he pulled the tumid and now dripping column from her aching jaws she began to spit the fluid out. She gulped back a series of shuddering breaths before her stomach heaved and she vomited rackingly onto the floor in front of her.

She did not open her eyes until she heard padding footsteps and then a door open and close. When finally she did open them she was alone in the neon glare, slumped in the corner by the pantry behind a puddle of regurgitated brandy laced with white streaks.

Her jaw ached. Her throat throbbed. Insofar as she was capable of coherent thought she thought that if the Russians were planning to rain missiles over America and Western Europe she wouldn't mind if they did it now.

'A LADY CALLED FROM England half an hour before,' the night clerk told Sidney Hunter, handing him his key, 'but she did not leave a message.'

Sidney thanked him. Why had she called again? Was she still worrying that a nuclear holocaust was bearing down on her, on humanity? Waiting for the lift and thinking about where he'd been half an hour ago, he felt guilty.

Sidney had not dined with one of his suppliers. He'd dined alone and then, as he had yesterday, had gone to a house in the Walletjes district and purchased an hour of the services of two nubile Dutch women. After a 'performance' involving striptease, cunnilingus and the use of a double dildo they had turned their attentions to Sidney.

Sidney had acquired his voyeuristic tastes in North Africa at the end of the War just before he was de-mobbed. In the Cairo shows there had been lesbianism and more: he'd seen women take on three men at a time or half a dozen in succession. He'd seen a woman fucked by a donkey.

Such exotic displays were not available in post-war Devon, although voyeurism was among the many tastes catered for in London, where the Hunters moved in 1950. But Sidney had applied two 'golden rules' to his marriage. He would only indulge his weakness on buying trips to Holland (which had begun before 1950). And he wouldn't allow himself to fantasize about the displays he'd witnessed abroad while he was per-forming his conjugal duties at home.

The lift arrived. Sidney entered and rode, sated and

contrite, to the fourth floor.

BERTRAND RUSSELL, BY now as well-known for his anti-nuclear campaigning as for his works of philosophy, had written to the Soviet Premier and the US President, condemning the one for his military adventurism and lauding the other for his efforts at appeasement. The warmonger was Kennedy, Khrushchev the peacemaker.

The President squeezed a few minutes into his bellicose schedule to compose a reply to Russell's letter:

> *'I think your attention might well be directed to the burglar rather than to those who caught the burglar.'*

FRIDAY

'Cuba will turn out to have been a blessing in sinister disguise.'

**DAILY MIRROR editorial,
26 October 1962**

MORNING

LAURENCE KNOCKED ON the door to the attic bedroom and entered. Andrew, a light sleeper, woke instantly in the elaborately canopied bed.

'Your ladyfriend has flown the coop,' Laurence announced. He held out a folded sheet of notepaper. Andrew took it, rubbed his eyes and read:

Dear Laurence and Andrew,

I've got to go to Sidney. I'm sorry.

Evelyn

He frowned. 'I assume she means the one in Holland, or has she misspelt the one in Australia? This Cuba affair does seem to be getting to her. Has something happened?'

Laurence shook his head. 'It's mainly good news. I had the wireless on while I was shaving. The Yanks have let an East German passenger ship through the blockade. Kennedy and Khrushchev have both responded positively to the appeals by – what's-his-name at the UN. But I doubt Evelyn heard the news before she left.'

'What time did she go?'

'Mrs Danvers heard a car start up about an hour ago. I suppose she's gone to Dover.' He sat on the end of the bed. 'Our Pilgrim's back, by the way. At least his motorbike's outside.' Andrew yawned. 'Do you want to go back to sleep?'

'No, I'll get up. Are you going in to work?'

'Needs must. Sarah too. Can you manage on your own? You may want to get out of the house. The cleaning ladies come in this morning and Mrs Danvers turns into her namesake.'

Andrew grinned. 'I remember!'

'It's very odd, but we seem to have had a ghostly visitation during the night. Someone – or something – came in and washed the kitchen floor.'

'Perhaps Sarah did it as a penance for recent impertinences.'

Laurence laughed. 'I doubt Sarah knows which is the business end of a mop! Why don't you get together with David again today?'

'I don't think there's much point. Really I ought to pay a duty call on the parentibus.'

'How's your father doing?'

'He can't speak properly since the second stroke.'

'Have the strokes mellowed him at all?'

'Not from Mother's point of view. He frets about the firm, doesn't trust his foremen to run it without him.'

'Is he still trying to squeeze the *Son* into *George Rutherford & Son*?'

'He did invite me to interior design some flats he was building last year, but I told him my Mayfair and Kensington ideas were a little "fast" for St Leonards. He's more tolerant now that I'm set up on my own. It was the window dressing he couldn't live with: "a pansy sort of job".'

Laurence stood up. 'I shan't worry about you today if you're returning to the family bosom. What about Evelyn? Should we be worrying about her?'

'If she really thinks we're on the brink of Armageddon, I suppose it makes sense to run to Sidney's stout chest – even if that means a trip to Amsterdam.'

FROM RYE TO HYTHE the road followed a serpentine route across the marshes. Traffic was heavy, often slowing to a horse-and-cart pace behind farm vehicles and lorries. Evelyn twice had to pull over and open the door and be sick, although by now she was only bringing up bile.

She couldn't get the taste of him out of her mouth.

WAITING FOR SARAH in the hall, Laurence heard sounds of hilarity from the kitchen. He went down the passageway and opened the kitchen door to find the cook red-faced with laughter at the sink, being squeezed from behind by a grinning Pilgrim who was dressed in his trademark jeans and tee shirt. Seated at the table opposite the housekeeper, the first of the cleaning women was also laughing. Even starchy Mrs Danvers was smiling. All their faces turned in Laurence's direction. The laughter subsided. Still grinning, Pilgrim slowly released the cook from his embrace. He looked a far cry from the sinister figure Laurence had seen from his window or the 'depraved' one that Evelyn had sensed. Was Evelyn as neurotic as Andrew seemed to imply, Laurence wondered. Was *he*?

'High jinks in here today,' he said, smiling to show no criticism was implied.

'Oh, this boy's such a card,' said Cook. She pulled up the skirt of her pinafore to pat her flushed face.

'So I see,' Laurence said. 'Where did you get to yesterday?' he asked Pilgrim. 'We were afraid you'd abandoned your young friend.'

'No risk of that. I had to go to London. See a man who owed us some money.'

'You went all the way to London?' Laurence said, as if the 150-mile round-trip were tantamount to crossing the Sahara. 'Where in London?'

'Hammersmith.'

'I see,' said Laurence, not that he did. 'Well' – he
tried to extricate himself without sounding officious –
'I'll leave you ladies to your high jinks. Don't keep them
from their work for too long,' he cautioned Pilgrim with
what he hoped was mock severity.

'He's just singing for his supper,' Cook said. 'Or for
his breakfast!' She began to giggle.

'Is he now,' said Laurence. 'You'll have to give him
a big one. Breakfast, I mean,' he added as he realized
how unfortunate his first suggestion was.

'Ooh, Mr Dickinson, you're as saucy as he is,' the
cook joshed him. Mrs Danvers pushed her chair back
and rose.

'I think that's enough merriment for one morning,'
she said.

ANDREW BREAKFASTED WITH Malcolm in the conservatory.

'Where's our other guest?' he asked Mrs Danvers
when she came in with the coffee pot.

'Gone to Hastings to get some fresh fish for dinner.
Such an obliging young man, he is.'

'I'm glad he's making himself useful,' Andrew said.
'Do you know Hastings?' he asked Malcolm as the
housekeeper left the conservatory. The boy smiled and
shook his head.

'My parents still live there,' Andrew went on,
allowing them to provide something to talk about. 'My
father's had a couple of strokes which have left him
semi-invalid. I don't get down very often, so I don't see
much of him, but my mother comes up to London for
the odd day or even a weekend. I wine and dine her,
take her to a concert or a play, give her a taste of the
High Life. My father lets her hire a nurse when she
comes to see me, but the rest of the time she has to
help with all the things he can't do for himself.'

To get off the depressing subject of his father,

whom he would be seeing all too soon, he asked: 'Do you live with your parents when you're at home?' Malcolm shook his head. 'Are they still alive?' Malcolm nodded. 'North of London? South of London? *In* London?'

Malcolm put one hand over the other and then raised it. 'North?' The boy nodded. 'North of Birmingham?' His hand went higher. 'North of Manchester?' Higher. 'North of the border?' Lower. Andrew knew Florence and Barcelona and Marrakech almost as well as he knew Hastings, but his domestic geography became hazy anywhere north of Regent's Park. He abandoned the guessing game and asked instead:

'Do you live with Pilgrim all the time?' Malcolm nodded.

'He isn't your *brother*, is he?' The boy smiled and shook his head.

'I can see he looks after you. Is he your boyfriend?' Malcolm shook his head again and, for the first time, frowned.

APPROACHING FOLKESTONE, EVELYN remembered where her passport was. It was in the safe in her bedroom in Hampstead Garden Suburb.

She sighed and looked for the next turn-off for the A20.

ANDREW PHONED FOR a taxi to his parents' house on the outskirts of Hastings. Not having warned her of his visit he found his mother pruning blackcurrant bushes at the bottom of the steeply shelved garden. It was a bright but cold morning. She was wearing an old cardigan, corduroy trousers and muddy brogues. Unmade-up, she looked tired and careworn, but her face lit up as he approached.

'Andrew! What a lovely surprise.'

'I'm staying at Laurence's for a couple of days with

Evelyn Hunter – you met her, remember?'

'Her husband helped you and Algie get started?'

He nodded. 'He's in Holland this week, buying diamonds. Actually, Evelyn's gone to join him today. She's
convinced the end of the world is at hand. You know:
this Cuba situation.'

'Well, if she's right I'm wasting my time out here!'
She laughed. 'I'm so behind with the garden this year.
Your father takes up all my time.'

'Is he any better?'

'He's coming along. Impatient as ever, of course.'
She smiled. 'He'll be pleased to see you. But let me
have you to myself for a bit. It seems ages since I saw
you. Tell me all your news.'

He told her what he'd bought for his flat since her
last visit, which new clients he and Algie had secured
and which new shows he'd seen in the West End. He
relayed some gossip about actors, politicians and
society people, not all of whose names were familiar to
her. Had she followed the Vassall trial? Only the
television news and the newspaper headlines. He told
her that his partner and Vassall had several mutual
acquaintances. His mother had met Algie, but so far as
he knew had not realized that his business partner was
homosexual. Homosexuality did not loom large in
Lillian Rutherford's circle of builders and bridge players
and golf club members.

'What about Fiona?' she asked. 'Are you still seeing
her?' Although Lillian had been introduced to Fiona
and to one of her predecessors, he had never brought
a girlfriend to Hastings.

'Yes, I'm still seeing her,' he said, 'though not for
much longer, I think.'

'Oh dear, what's wrong with this one?'

He shrugged. 'Nothing particularly. You know me.'
As always when he made this kind of casual self-
deprecating remark, he was aware that she did not

know him at all, that at the core of their ostensibly close relationship lay the Big Secret of his homosexual past. 'I like to – move on after a while,' he added; this at least was honest.

'No wedding bells in the offing then?' She said this lightly but he knew she yearned to see him settled. Maybe it was in reaction to this that he now chose to announce, woundingly, something to which he had only given an occasional passing thought. He shook his head. 'I've been thinking I may go and live abroad,' he said.

Lillian had resumed her pruning. Now she stopped and looked at him across the top of a blackcurrant bush. 'Oh, what's brought this on?'

He shrugged again. 'I just feel I'm about finished with England.' Saying this, it felt like the truth.

'Where are you thinking of going?'

'I'm not sure. Italy maybe.' He more or less named the first country that came into his head. 'There are some exciting things going on in interior design there.' This was equally true of Finland and, to a lesser extent, of West Berlin or even West London.

'Is that what you want to concentrate on?'

'Well, I'm a bit fed up with shop windows and posters.' This he knew to be true. 'Will you mind?'

She stared into his eyes. 'Will I mind if you go away? Of course I'll mind, but if it's what you want you must do it.'

Trying to sell the idea to himself as much as to her, he described the work of some leading designers he had seen in homes, shops and magazines in London and, last spring, in Rome. 'Are you sure you won't mind?' he asked her again, as if emigration were already a fact rather than a fancy.

'It's your life,' she said; 'you must lead it your own way. We'd better go in and see your dad.'

As they walked up the garden she showed him

what she had planted for next year, what she had dug up, what she planned. To Andrew this cycle of planting and culling that featured so large in his mother's life and Laurence's was part of the provincial suffocation that he had fled three years ago. His London penthouse did not boast so much as a window-box. In the kitchen he waited while she removed her brogues, then waited while she made cups of instant coffee.

'George, look what the cat's brought in!' she exclaimed as Andrew followed her into the lounge-dining-room, where his father sat in a wheelchair at the dining table on which a large jigsaw-puzzle lay half-completed.

'Hello, Dad,' Andrew said.

'Gnllo,' replied his father with a lopsided smile. This was the third time Andrew had seen him since the first stroke, and it was still unnerving. Always a burly man, like Laurence, the strokes seemed to have diminished him. The initial stroke had left him paralysed down one side of his body and speechless, although a degree of articulacy had returned within days. He battled against his slurred speech with the same vigour with which he'd earlier confronted Andrew's teenage 'rebellion'. As soon as Andrew started at Hastings Grammar it became obvious to his teachers – and to Lillian – that a boy with a flair for Modern Languages and Art was never likely to take up bricklaying or even one of the building trade's loftier opportunities (although, ironically, Interior Design now seemed to be his ultimate goal); but to George their son's adamant refusal, even on school holidays, to become part of the already second-generation family firm remained for many years a bitter pill, a betrayal.

At least today his temper was in check. The recent second stroke had clearly set him back. Prompted by his mother, Andrew retold the progress of his business and his flat. His father grunted comments and questions which Lillian was usually able to translate. He slurped his coffee from the spout of a child's plastic beaker held in his good hand. Remembering that Sarah had asked Laurence to convert his precious rose garden into a tennis court, Andrew managed to extract some conversation from this topic. Neither he nor his mother said anything about the possibility of his leaving the country.

His father shook his hand limply and said goodbye – 'Gnoo-gye' – with another lopsided grin. Lillian drove him down to Laurence's hotel on the seafront. She couldn't leave George long enough to stay for lunch, but she drank a gin-and-tonic with Andrew and Laurence in the hotel bar. She and Laurence had many mutual acquaintances, particularly in the town hall: prior to his strokes George had been an alderman. Smoking a cigarette, listening to their local gossip, Andrew allowed the notion of emigrating to take on more solid shape in his mind.

He walked his mother back to her car. He saw tears in her eyes as she kissed him goodbye. 'Come down again,' she said. 'Don't leave it so long next time.'

'You're always welcome in Kensington,' he told her.

'It's not easy to get away. I'd be afraid now that – something might happen while I wasn't here.'

He kissed her in the Continental manner, on both cheeks. 'I'll try to get down again very soon,' he promised, both meaning it and dreading it.

AFTERNOON

HOME, SAFE AT last, in Kingsley Way, the first thing Evelyn did was to clean her teeth, vigorously, for the sixth or seventh time since last night. The house felt cold and unwelcoming. She turned the heating on and lit the gas fire in the living-room. Then she telephoned Sidney's travel agent, who told her the rest of the day's flights to Amsterdam were fully booked; she'd tried to book for another customer.

'Could I get there by train and ferry?'

'There's an overnight crossing from Harwich to the Hook of Holland. Or you could go Dover–Ostend from Victoria and change in Brussels.'

'This Cuba business has got me so I don't know what to do for the best,' Evelyn confessed.

'Me too!' the woman exclaimed. 'I've been bringing all my jewellery with me to the office. You know, in case the Russians start to bomb us. Then, if I survive the bombs I can use my jewellery to buy food for the first few weeks.'

There was no relief in finding someone who shared her sense of doom. Evelyn thanked her and hung up. Going to Amsterdam seemed like an ordeal. Perhaps she would just stay here until Sid returned on Sunday. If the Russians blew London to bits, she would face oblivion on her own. After last night the prospect of oblivion was still attractive.

She went to see if the water was hot enough for a decontaminating bath.

'SO HOW WERE things at home?' Laurence asked as Andrew joined him in the hotel restaurant.

'Pretty ghastly. Dad making these gurgling noises when he tries to speak. It's strange to find myself pitying someone I resented for so many years.'

Laurence chose not to retread the path of Andrew's long feud with his father. 'Your mother looks worn out. Will she be able to go on coping?'

'I'm sure she will. She comes from tough stock. My grandmother scrubbed floors and took in washing to pay for Mother's private schooling.' He scanned the menu. 'Did you solve the mystery of your phantom floor-cleaner?'

Laurence shook his head. 'No. I expect Cook did it before she went home yesterday and Mrs Danvers didn't notice.' The head waiter came to take their order. Laurence counted heads in the half-full restaurant. At this time of year the hotel had few guests but the restaurant enjoyed good business from the local middle classes. Sarah was sitting at a table with one of the receptionists.

'I don't quite know why,' Andrew said as the maître-d' retreated, 'but I suddenly told my mother I'm thinking of going abroad to live.'

'Anywhere in particular?'

'I told her Italy, I suppose because I was in Rome at Whitsun and liked what I saw in furniture and interiors.'

'But you're not seriously thinking of emigrating, are you? It wouldn't be very fair on Algie.' Laurence had met Andrew's partner who in his still-talked-of heyday had painted commissioned portraits of nobles and celebrities. But the years and a weakness for pink gin had atrophied his talent. Apart from a few Beardsley-esque posters for obscure chamber musicians his duties at the agency were chiefly confined to administration. It was Andrew, with a flair for modernistically simple and imaginative design, who was the mainstay

THE BEXHILL MISSILE CRISIS

of the firm.

'Oh, Algie could easily replace me,' Andrew said. 'London's full of window dressers with delusions of grandeur.'

'Could you compete with Italian designers on their own territory? Would they let you?'

'It doesn't have to be Italy. I could follow your example and invest my "talent" in Spain. Madrid's got moneyed people with pretensions in fashion and style. Barcelona's more fun, of course: all that glorious Gaudí. Maybe it's time I had a Brett Ashley phase,' he laughed, 'you know, get tanked up with the expatriate set, screw a matador or two!'

'I thought you left that sort of behaviour on – what is it you call it? – "the other side of the bridge",' Laurence said. 'Not thinking of "reconverting", are you?'

'Oh, I sometimes feel the pull of the old life – the murky water below the bridge.' The head waiter returned with their wine. When the ritual of tasting and pouring was completed, Laurence said:

'When you refer to your past life as murky water under the bridge, does that include me – and David Yates?'

'Of course not. You and David are about the only *un*-murky things I look back on.' Andrew toasted him and drank some wine. 'It's all the rest of it. Lorenzo, you've only ever paddled in the shallows of that metaphorical river through the Queer World, you've never really swum out where the water is deep and dangerous.'

'And what have I missed?'

'Do you really want to know?'

'Obviously, or I wouldn't ask.'

Andrew lit a cigarette before going on. 'You've missed being sucked off in smelly urinals with little or no light; the metal ones are known as "iron lungs"! You've missed midnight daisy chains on Hampstead

Heath and the Putney towpath. You've missed parties, quietly advertised by word of mouth, where all the guests join in a big orgy. You've missed boy brothels in Berlin and Tangier – in Tangier they cost about ten shillings each, or for just five bob you can watch the other clients having their fun. If you'd like more details on any of this, you have only to ask.' He leaned back and inhaled deeply on his cigarette.

Laurence made an effort not to look provincial and prudish. 'You're right,' he said. 'I've missed out on those things, although I have heard of most of them before. Even Bexhill has "cottage queens" and I'm told there are boy renters here in Hastings! But queer life doesn't have to be like that. If it is, if it *was*, it's because you *chose* it.'

'I never saw it as a conscious choice until I chose to walk away from it.'

'I've never quite grasped exactly why you did walk away from it.'

Andrew sighed. 'Working with Algie had a lot to do with it. And the other queens when we worked in Selfridges: always talking about last night's "trade", the places they'd "cruised". Being older Algie has to resort to picking up renters, or he fumbles with the other sad old queens in some of the dingier cottages.'

Laurence smiled. 'I suppose my new chauffeur's going to be a sort of salaried renter – *if* he gets here and *if* he's interested. Does that make *me* one of your sad old queens?'

Andrew shook his head. 'No, because you won't be broken-hearted if he doesn't turn up and you won't send him packing if he turns up but doesn't "come across". There's more to your life than the next piece of trade – and to mine too, I hope. But Algie's drinking more heavily than ever and one of these days he'll use the booze to wash down a few sleeping pills. It was seeing him as what I might turn into that made me decide to try my luck on the "other side of the bridge".'

'But you've already admitted that you're no happier over there.' A waiter approached with their first course. Laurence leaned back as the plate was placed in front of him. 'I think it's not so much which side of the bridge you're on,' he said; 'it's the quality of the water that counts. Perhaps you *should* go and live abroad. Maybe it's time you jumped into a different river.'

'Perhaps I should,' Andrew said, stubbing out his cigarette and picking up his fork. 'Or perhaps' – he laughed – 'I need to be pushed!'

AFTER LUNCH THEY took Sarah home with them. It was now raining, a heavier downpour than yesterday's. 'I'm going to Ruth's,' Sarah announced as they turned into the drive. 'I'll take Malcolm. We can play Monopoly or something.'

'Take Pilgrim too,' her father said. 'If he hasn't done another vanishing act. His bike's not here. Andrew, you can go with them or you can come with me to East-bourne. Today's the day I take Mrs Danvers to visit her mother in a nursing home.'

'I've had enough invalids for one day,' Andrew said. 'And I'll pass on the Monopoly too. I see enough of Oxford Street and Regent Street when I'm working. Don't worry about me. I'll curl up on a sofa with *The Pumpkin Eater*. Mrs Mortimer's giving me off-putting insights into married life – much as your mother has, Sarah!'

'You'll have the house to yourself,' Laurence told him. 'The cleaning ladies will have gone and it's Cook's afternoon off.'

The housekeeper reported that Pilgrim had gone to Dover to find out about the ferries. 'He only needed to phone,' Laurence said. I suppose he'll be back here to sleep, if not for dinner. I think I'll send the pair of them on their way tomorrow.'

'Malcolm's still recuperating,' Sarah protested.

'If he's fit enough to drive around in your car, he's fit enough to ride pillion on a motorcycle,' her father said. He went to change before driving the housekeeper to Eastbourne. Sarah went to find Malcolm. Andrew went to the music room and put an LP of Mozart's 'Jupiter' Symphony on the bulky Grundig gramophone before sprawling on a settee with the Penelope Mortimer novel. The book and the music sent him rapidly to sleep.

EVELYN WAS ALSO lying on a sofa listening to music. The sofa was in her lounge, the gramophone was a Ferguson and the LP was an album of film themes played by Mantovani's orchestra with Rawicz & Landauer. It was a record that usually made her weep for the romance that had perished in her life when Tony's Lancaster plummeted into a field outside Berlin. After a nostalgic wallow she would pull herself together and get on with something practical like preparing her husband's dinner or ironing his shirts.

But today the soaring strings and pounding pianos only seemed to mock her, underscoring her hollow marriage, her empty existence. Three years of listening to Andrew over occasional lunches and dinners had led her to imagine that what her life lacked was sex: ground-breaking, earth-shaking sex. In five minutes – less – on the floor of Laurence's kitchen Pilgrim had not just degraded her; he had taught her a lesson. Her mother's generation were right: sex was just a dirty business that women had to put up with because men needed it. It was only in books, written by *men*, that women got pleasure out of being violated.

The female orgasm was no more than a myth put about by men to justify the filthy things they liked to make women do. If she had been made to do what Pilgrim had made her do by someone to whom she was physically attracted – Tony, the German in Torquay or (most inconceivable of all) Sidney – the degradation would have been only marginally less.

She had to face the fact that what she had in life was all she would ever have, all there was to life. This sobering thought enabled her to feel a bit calmer about last night's experience. But she couldn't decide whether or not she should go to Amsterdam.

And in this uncertain, not-quite-calm state she dozed off.

THE NURSING HOME, in Eastbourne's affluent Meads district, was from the 1930s, the same era as Laurence's house, and in the same mock-Tudor style. He snoozed in the Bentley while his housekeeper visited her mother who was in robust physical health for an 86-year-old but far advanced in senility. Mrs Danvers stayed for only half-an-hour and was in a state of distress when she returned to the car.

'One of her bad days, is it?' he asked.

'She called me "Mother".' Mrs Danvers began to cry. 'She thinks I'm her mother. My grandmother died in the 'flu epidemic in 1918.'

He patted her arm. 'Now, Olive, don't upset yourself.' These grim fortnightly excursions were among the rare times when they used each other's first names, although she could never quite bring herself to drop the 'Mister'.

'Oh, Mr Laurence,' she sobbed, 'I just wish it could be over, and I know that's a wicked thing to say.' He started the engine and reversed out of the drive.

'We'll go to Bondolfi's,' he said. This was Mrs Danvers' favourite watering hole, a chocolatier near the town centre whose tearoom served gooey cakes and the crumbliest pastries. She blew her nose.

'You spoil me, Mr Laurence,' she said.

A HEAVY WEIGHT ON his chest woke Andrew. Something slapped against his face. He opened his eyes groggily. Pilgrim was straddling him in a kneeling position. He was naked. His clothes were piled carelessly on the floor beside the sofa. His semi-erect penis was slapping against Andrew's face.

'Wake up, Sleeping Beauty,' he said. 'You've got work to do.' His large white teeth gleamed down at Andrew above his pale hairless torso and the long thick penis which almost filled Andrew's vision. Pilgrim's body smelt, not overpoweringly, of sweat. His penis, perhaps last washed yesterday night, had a gamey odour – an odour from the world Andrew had left two and a half years ago, an odour that was the opposite of repellent: enticing, almost intoxicating.

'Get off me,' he said. He struggled to free himself but his arms were trapped under Pilgrim's powerful thighs. 'Someone could walk in any minute.'

'They're all out,' Pilgrim said.

'They could be back any time.'

'Then you'd better get on with it.' He lifted himself off Andrew's chest, shifting all his weight onto his knees and pushed his penis, now fully erect, against Andrew's mouth.

Andrew's arms were now free. He could wriggle himself clear or push Pilgrim off. He did neither. He ran his tongue, experimentally, down the taut marbled shaft. Grasping it with one hand, he licked the heart-shaped head and slowly sucked the entire organ into his mouth. With his other hand he played with Pilgrim's heavy dangling balls. Then, as Pilgrim lifted himself out of Andrew's compliant mouth and leaned forward, Andrew began to lick his balls, rolling each of them in his mouth. Pilgrim lifted himself higher, so that Andrew's tongue could explore the ginger-furred folds behind his scrotum.

Without touching himself Andrew, still fully dressed,

came inside his clothes. He gasped. His tongue continued to probe. Pilgrim tensed, lowered himself a fraction onto Andrew's face, sniggered and then farted. It was a loud fart that reeked of the compost heap, of the graveyard. Pilgrim laughed as Andrew gagged and pushed the other off him. Crashing onto the floor beside the sofa, Pilgrim lay there, laughing hysterically, as Andrew bounded off the sofa and ran out of the room, still gagging. The sound of his laughter followed Andrew up two flights of stairs to the attic bedroom.

IT WAS A BORING afternoon at the Yates's. Ruth had left instructions that she was not to be woken before six. Her sister-in-law had also taken to her bed, leaving her son in the care of his father and grandparents.

'Shall we go for a drive instead?' Sarah had proposed. Malcolm had shaken his head and got down onto the floor with Nigel. Sarah endured two hours of watching four males, aged from three to sixty-three, play tiddlywinks and other similar games interrupted by regular snacks and beverages served by Mrs Yates Senior.

The rain was slackening when Sarah was finally able to drag Malcolm off to her car. 'Shall we go and park in the woods?' she suggested. He shook his head again. She wished she'd just driven him to the woods without asking.

Pilgrim's motorcycle was back in front of the garage, dripping wet. Malcolm headed straight for the flat over the garage before she could invite him up to her own rooms.

After a long soak in a bubble bath Sarah was still feeling on edge and impatient for a more protracted induction into the world of adult sex. She went along the landing in her bathrobe. Malcolm's room was as he had left it when she'd summoned him to the Yates's earlier, the bed made, two towels neatly folded over the bedrail. It looked like an unlet room in one of her father's hotels. Going back to her own rooms she dressed before venturing out to the garage, unsure as to whether or how she would be able to inveigle Malcolm away from Pilgrim but resolved to try.

The rain had stopped, although the sky was thick with low dark clouds. The motorbike was gone but lights were on upstairs. She went up the stairs, knocked and entered. Other than an unmade bed and a trail of discarded towels there was no sign of occupation. The two panniers from the motorcycle had gone, and so had Malcolm's guitar which she had never heard him play. The visitors were not out, they had departed, unceremoniously. She would have to look elsewhere for her second shagging.

Her father's car entered the drive as she turned to descend the stairs.

EVENING

'WHAT A SHAME,' ANDREW said when Laurence brought the news, with a gin-and-tonic, to his room in the attic. 'Just as we were getting attached to them.'

'Malcolm maybe,' Laurence admitted; 'he's quite endearing, but we're hardly going to miss Pilgrim, are we?' He sat down on the bed.

'Speak for yourself. Pilgrim and I became very close this afternoon. I dozed off in the music room and woke up to find him trying to push his cock down my throat.'

'My God! What did you do?'

Andrew knotted his tie in front of a mirror whose frame was an elaborate wooden Arabesque. 'There seemed to be only one thing *to* do: I sucked it.'

'Did you, by golly.' Laurence gave a short barking laugh. 'I hope he hasn't set you back, so to speak.'

Andrew gave his reflection – or Laurence's – a wry smile. 'Perhaps I shall end up like you, plying both ends of the bridge, "so to speak".'

Laurence acknowledged the italicized tribute with a smile of his own. 'I don't think "plying" is the word for what I do.' He paused. 'I suppose I ought to mention that I had – I'm not sure it qualifies to be called an "experience" with Pilgrim on Tuesday night.'

'I'm all agog.' Andrew perched on the other side of the bed with careful attention to his trouser creases.

'When I went to bed after our talk I looked out my window and he was sitting stark naked in front of the garage flat window with the light on – tossing himself off.'

'Is that all? You didn't rush over and offer to lend a hand?'

Laurence laughed again. 'I might have done if it had been the other one – Malcolm, although his appeal is more in the area of cuddling than mutual mastur-bation.' He affected not to notice Andrew's arched eye-brows and went on:

'But I mean, imagine if Mrs Danvers had looked out and seen him. Or Evelyn.'

Andrew laughed and said: 'Mrs D. would have fainted. I fear Evelyn would just close her curtains!'

Laurence did not laugh. 'It's weird,' he went on, 'but I had the strangest sensation that he *knew* I was watching, that he was doing it for my benefit. Probably because of that I made a point of asking Sarah if he tried anything with her while they were in Brighton on Wednesday. She said no. But do you think he might have?'

'Well, it's not something I'd admit to *my* father!' Andrew said.

Laurence stood up abruptly. 'I'm going to get the truth out of her.'

His daughter looked up crossly from the television in her small sitting room as he knocked and entered. She was watching *Six-Five Special*.

'Go away. You know I always watch this.'

Laurence turned the volume down. 'Sarah. This is important. When you told me Pilgrim didn't try anything on in Brighton the other day – was that the truth?'

Sarah continued to watch the TV screen, on which Cliff Richard was faintly singing 'It'll Be Me'. 'What does it matter now? He's gone. They've both gone.'

'I insist you tell me if something happened.'

She looked at him. Her colour rose. 'All right. I stopped outside Pevensey because the engine over-heated, and he got out to pee in a field and then he showed me his – thing.'

'The dirty *bastard*!' Laurence raged. 'You didn't let him – *do* anything, did you?'

'If you must know, I gave him a ...' As with Ruth she pantomimed what she had done to Pilgrim. Laurence looked aghast.

'Sarah! My God –' Words failed him. This was an aspect of being a parent that he hadn't had to face before.

'He wasn't the first I've done it to and he's unlikely to be the last,' she went on defiantly. Her blush faded as her father's colour deepened.

'Who else have you done it to?' he demanded. Aware that confrontation was her best defence against any probing of her other, darker secret, Sarah brazen-ed it out:

'Laurence – *Dad* – I'm eighteen. This is what eighteen-year-olds do in parked cars.'

'Not in my day they didn't.'

'Maybe *you* didn't, but I bet *Mother* did.'

'*Fuck* your bloody Mother!' Laurence exploded.

'Somebody will have to,' Sarah said with a grin. Her father, despite his anger, laughed grimly.

'SID?'

'Hello, dear. I was just going out for dinner. How's the weather in Bexhill? It's raining buckets here.'

'I'm not in Bexhill. I've come home.'

'I thought you were staying till Sunday.'

'Well, I'm not ... I thought I might come out to Holland after all. Just for the weekend.'

In Amsterdam Sidney Hunter sighed. 'There's no point doing that. I'm going to be in Rotterdam all day tomorrow, and there may still be people I need to see on Sunday, before I come home.'

'I just want to be with you – you know, in case something happens. This trouble in Cuba.'

'Has anything happened today? I haven't even read yesterday's paper.'

'I've got the news on now. The Americans stopped and searched a cargo ship that the Russians had chartered.'

'Did they find what they were looking for?'

'Well, no. I suppose the boats that turned back were the ones with the missiles and stuff. But the Americans say their spy planes show that there's still work going on at the missile sites in Cuba. And Khrushchev has banned Western diplomats from travelling outside Moscow, which must mean there's something they don't want them to see.'

'This is going to drag on for weeks. Months. We've got to get on with our lives, Evelyn.'

'But I don't want to be alone. I want to be with you,' she repeated. A part of her mind held the thought that if she went to Amsterdam he might try to make love to her. She did not want ever to be touched by a man, any man – not even by Sidney – or at least not for a very long time. Another sigh came down the line.

'Then why did you leave Bexhill? You should go back, Evelyn.'

'I can't,' she wailed.

'Don't be silly. Of course you can. I'm sure Andrew and his friend will do a better job of keeping your mind off things than I can.'

'IT'S LUCKY FOR him that he's gone,' Laurence remarked to Andrew as they went downstairs. 'If Sarah had told me this yesterday, I'd have killed the filthy bloody swine.'

'I believe you would,' Andrew said. 'In which case I'd have missed out on my ordeal this afternoon.'

'Are you planning to give me a more detailed version of this encounter?'

Andrew shook his head as they went into the lounge. 'I don't think so.'

Laurence took their glasses over to the cocktail cabinet. 'Could Pilgrim have had anything to do with Evelyn leaving?'

'He still wasn't back from his jaunt to London when we all went to bed, was he? Unless something happened during the night.'

'Surely he wouldn't have dared to go to her room? And even if he had, she'd have called out and woken us up.'

'Has he been through *all* of us like a dose of salts?' Andrew speculated, raising his eyebrows. 'Mrs Danvers told me this morning how obliging he was. You'd better ask her precisely what she means by "obliging"!'

'I did catch him giving Cook a cuddle in the kitchen,' Laurence said. They laughed. The telephone rang in the next room. Laurence went to answer it. Andrew picked up his glass and followed him, lounging against the study door jamb.

'Hello?' Laurence said into the receiver. '... Ah, Evelyn. We were just wondering about you. Are you all right? How's the weather in Amsterdam?'

THE *MARUCLA* WAS an American-built liberty ship,
Panamanian owned, Lebanese registered, on charter
to the Soviets out of the Baltic port of Riga. It was stopped at seven a.m., Eastern Standard Time, on Friday
and boarded at eight by men from two US destroyers,
the *John Pierce* and the *Joseph P. Kennedy, Jr.*
(named after the President's elder brother, a Navy pilot
killed during World War Two). The crew of the *Marucla*
offered no resistance. The searchers found no wea-
pons and the supply ship was permitted to resume her
voyage.

By selecting a foreign-owned vessel as the first to
be boarded at the blockade, Kennedy was diluting the
provocation to the Russians. But he was also making
the point that the quarantine had teeth. In light of the
discovery that the Soviets had stepped up work both
on the missile sites and the assembly of Ilyushin IL-28
bomber aircraft, the President ordered the low-level
U-2 overflights of Cuba to be stepped up from twice a
day to every two hours.

That afternoon Khrushchev sent a rambling,
emotional message over the 'hot line' which the White
House received at six p.m. The final paragraph began:

> *'If you have not lost your self-control and*
> *sensibly conceive what this might lead to,*
> *then, Mr President, we and you ought not*
> *to pull on the ends of the rope in which you*
> *have tied the knot of war, because the*
> *more the two of us pull, the tighter that knot*
> *will be tied.'*

SATURDAY

'IT'S BOILING UP AGAIN ALL OVER'

**DAILY SKETCH, 27 October 1962,
front-page headline**

MORNING

SARAH SPREAD A SMEAR of marmalade over unbuttered toast. Acne was a constant enemy; look at Ruth. 'I thought you weren't going to Brighton this week,' she said.

'So did I,' her father replied, 'but something's come up, and now I need to.' The rooks were pecking at the heavily fertilized soil near his roses. Laurence contemplated fetching his shotgun but settled for banging on the conservatory window, which they ignored.

'But why do *I* have to come with you?'

'I want you where I can keep an eye on you.'

'I hope you're not going to start treating me like a child again,' she pouted.

'I'm treating you like a delinquent,' Laurence said, still watching the rooks. 'Which is what you are.'

'That Banqueting woman hates having me in her office.'

'You're not going to be in Banqueting. You're going to be on Reception. You're going to learn *all* about the hotel business, not just the bits you like.'

'Oh God,' Sarah said.

EVELYN HEADED SOUTH on the A21. This is a mistake, she thought. I shouldn't be going anywhere near Bexhill.

She had fallen, in Bexhill, into the clutches of something that wished to harm her, to bring her down to its own subhuman level. Yesterday she had fled the scene of her ravishing. Today she was returning. Was she not mad!

Her ravisher had left for good this time, Laurence had assured her last night, taking poor little Malcolm with him. Between them Laurence and Andrew and Sidney had browbeaten her into going back to Sussex. Andrew was hardly a rock to cling to in this most violent of storms, but Laurence possessed some of her husband's solidness and stability. And there was a kind of comfort in the fact that the housekeeper shared Evelyn's sense that the crisis in Cuba was all too likely to turn into a catastrophe. But going back to that house – it *was* madness.

At least, with Malcolm gone, she would have no reason to revisit the kitchen.

Her every instinct, still, was to turn round and go home to safe suburban Kingsley Way – even if Khrushchev might be about to turn it into a radioactive wasteland.

LAURENCE TOOK THE A27 to Brighton. Sarah pretended to read the *New Musical Express*. She too was thinking about Pilgrim and Malcolm. Yes, Malcolm had taken her virginity, enabling her to score points over Ruth and most of their tennis and house-party set, but somehow she didn't feel that she'd been really and truly – properly! – *screwed* (her mother's verb came into her mind rather than the Anglo-Saxon one). She should have done it with Pilgrim. She should have done it with 'Sharlz'.

She mentally 'inventoried' the boys at the Tennis Club, the ones she had *not* masturbated in the back of a car as well as those she had. *Which of them shall I screw with first?* she wondered.

And then it occurred to her that she would probably, over the coming weeks and months, screw with *all* of them.

BESIDE HER AT the wheel Laurence was also thinking different thoughts about Malcolm and Pilgrim.

He fretted about Malcolm, seemingly so innocent and vulnerable, trapped in the company of Pilgrim. If only Pilgrim had simply not returned from his jaunts on Thursday or Friday. Laurence could have paid for Malcolm to go to a special school, learn to read and write. Surely some job could be found for him in one of the hotels. He could be – almost – the son Laurence had once yearned for. After last night Malcolm seemed to Laurence a more deserving prospect than his unruly daughter.

He had been wrong to think of Pilgrim as some sort of sinister, malevolent figure. He'd turned out to be closer to the 'monster of depravity' Andrew had teased Evelyn with – just another sexual hooligan in this ugly modern world that Sarah was so greedily inheriting. It was not the world for which Laurence had fought and Derek died.

It would almost serve this world right if Kennedy and Khrushchev between them blew it to smithereens.

EVEN ANDREW WAS not his usual unruffled self as he showered and shaved and then breakfasted, alone, in the conservatory. He ignored the two morning papers laid out beside the coffee-pot.

His mind continued to review his humiliation at Pilgrim's hands yesterday afternoon. He'd made a joke of it to Laurence, omitting the degrading climax which, like the filthiest of filthy jokes, was not in the least bit funny. Yesterday he had told Laurence some of the sleazier facts of life in the Queer World, but he would never tell Laurence – or anybody – about Pilgrim farting in his face. He could almost still smell the stench that had driven him from the music room, from the confrontation with his Past that increasingly this week had come to seem more present than past, a process begun by David and Laurence which Pilgrim had yesterday consolidated.

'Pilgrim'. Such an ambiguous name; such an ambiguous individual! Was this his particular 'crusade': to force the people he came into contact with to confront their true nature, to face up to the things they had been running away from?

Psychological twaddle! he told himself sternly. And defying the 'demons' of both yesterday and yesteryear, he spent the morning in the music room finishing *The Pumpkin Eater* while he waited for Evelyn to arrive. He hoped the novel might give him further insights into the kind of woman Evelyn was.

It did not. Getting pregnant – if it were even possible with her gynaecological history – was unlikely to solve Evelyn's problem. Ironically, Pilgrim may have hit the nail on the head when he prescribed her 'a good shag'.

Within minutes of finishing the book he heard her car pull up outside.

EVELYN APPROACHED THE front door with an emotion that was close to dread. She avoided looking up at the window over the garage, fearful that despite their assurances she might see Pilgrim there. It would not have surprised her – would, indeed, have confirmed her deepest apprehensions – if the opening front door revealed him standing there, naked, massive, threatening.

In fact, of course, it was Mrs Danvers, in another of her dark-blue dresses that was almost a uniform, who greeted her with a smile of reassuring warmth.

'Mrs Hunter, we're *so* glad to have you back.'

But to Evelyn it still felt like a mistake to be here.

AFTERNOON

'WE'RE INTO THE Last Days,' the woman in the cloche hat proclaimed loudly. 'It was forecast in the Book of Revelations. The Antichrist has opened Pandora's Box and let loose the Four Horsemen of the Apocalypse. War, Famine, Plague and Pestilence.' She sipped her sherry. As well as the cloche hat she was wearing a tweed suit, a collar and tie and stout walking shoes.

'Aren't plague and pestilence the same thing?' queried the barman.

'There are important differences,' she informed him but did not elaborate. She downed the rest of her sherry and headed with a determined stride towards the door and her next destination – or destiny. The barman caught Andrew's eye and twirled one finger against the side of his head in a familiar gesture.

'A rather mixed bag of mythology,' Andrew commented to Evelyn. 'I don't remember Pandora's Box being a horsebox.'

'She's right in principle,' Evelyn said, toying nervously with her jade bracelet. 'If Russia and the USA do start fighting, it will mean the end of everything.'

'We'd better have another drink.' Andrew raised a finger to summon the barman to their end of the bar.

THE PUB WAS near a village where, Andrew said, his grandmother used to live. After a lunch of soup and sandwiches he directed her north again on the A267. 'Turn left here,' he said after ten minutes.

'Andrew, I said no country lanes. It's barely the width of the car.'

'It's only half a mile. This time of year there won't be anybody else.'

Evelyn steered gingerly into the narrow lane which was muddy with mossy banks and high blackthorn hedges. 'I don't want to have any more unfortunate – encounters.'

'I take full responsibility for bringing Pilgrim and Malcolm – or should I say Pilgrim and mayhem? – into our lives.'

The Renault stalled as Evelyn's foot slipped off the clutch pedal. 'I don't want to talk about them. Him.'

'I honestly think we should,' he said, looking at her with an expression that no longer mocked or teased.

'Not here, not now,' she pleaded.

'All right, darling.'

'And don't keep calling me darling. I'm *not* your darling.' She restarted the engine.

'Evelyn.' He put an arm round her shoulders but she shook it off.

'Leave me alone.'

The lane ended with a widening of the banks on the edge of a wood of oak and beech and pine trees. Evelyn turned off the engine. They lit cigarettes. Evelyn checked her make-up in the rear-view mirror.

'If it makes it any easier,' he said, 'you're not the only one who's had a bit of bother from Pilgrim.'

'"A bit of bother?"' she echoed, still studying her reflection: *who is this woman? and where is she going?* 'A bit more than a bit of bother.'

'He exposed himself to Sarah in her car the other evening.'

'She was obviously leading him on.'

'Maybe so, but Laurence certainly didn't encourage him, and neither did I.'

She turned to look at him in amazement. 'He – exposed himself to you and Laurence?'

'Laurence got a sort of exhibition. I' – he hesitated –

'was treated to rather more than that. What about you?'

Evelyn turned her head away. 'I can't talk about it. It was too disgusting. He made me – no, I can't talk about it.' She inhaled so deeply that she started coughing. After yesterday's showers she had kept the Renault's canopy up, although it was sunny today; Andrew wound his window down further to let the smoke out. When she stopped coughing she blurted:

'He said you were – queer, but if he exposed himself to Laurence and – did something to you, *he* must be the one who's queer, mustn't he? But then, why me – and Sarah?'

'It's more complicated than that. Humiliating people – male or female – seems to be the object of his game.'

'*Game*? You think it's just a game?'

'To Pilgrim it is. He's very good at it.' He gave a brief sardonic laugh. 'Did you tell Sid about him?'

'I'll never be able to tell Sid.'

'Presumably they're out of the country by now,' he said. 'I wonder why Malcolm stays with him. But they're bound to be back sooner or later. We ought to put a stop to him. Pilgrim. You could go to the police.'

'I could no more tell a policeman than I could tell Sid. Not even a police*woman*. Why don't *you* tell them?'

He blew smoke through the open window. 'Queers tend to steer clear of the police. Don't forget it's illegal even to be queer.'

Evelyn crushed her cigarette into the ashtray. 'So he was right about you, was he? You are – that way?'

Andrew smiled at her circumlocution. 'I used to be. I thought I'd given it up, but Pilgrim seems to have reminded me that the possibility will always be there. Like giving up smoking.' He inhaled with mock defiance.

'What makes people – queer?'

Andrew grimaced. 'I saw a joke about that on a

lavatory wall once. Someone had written, "*My mother made me a homosexual*", and underneath somebody else wrote, "*If I pay for the wool, will she make me one*"!'

Evelyn smiled thinly. 'Is that what causes it? Did you and Algie have mothers who were too possessive?'

'That's one theory, but I'm not sure that it matters how or why.' He threw his cigarette end into a puddle. 'I've never liked the way so many queers act as if Fate has dealt them an especially cruel hand. There must be just as much potential loneliness and unhappiness for someone crippled or disfigured, or even for someone who's just a widower or an old maid on the shelf.'

'Even for some married women,' she said bitterly. They fell silent for a few moments.

'Shall we go for a walk now that we're here?' he suggested. 'Or will it ruin your shoes?'

'I came prepared for the country this time,' she said. 'I've got my galoshes in the back.'

The overshoes made a comical contrast with her calf-length Selfridges mink coat and apricot-coloured linen suit from Fenwick's. Andrew too presented a Kensington version of rural life: ankle-length khaki Burberry raincoat, a beige cashmere roll-neck sweater and fawn cavalry-twill trousers from Cecil Gee, leather shoes from Florence.

'We may be a little overdressed for a nature ramble,' he said as they set off down the mud-puddled track.

MORE THAN A WOOD, it was a small forest. Watery sunlight dappled the tree trunks and their green and brown leaves. After two days of rain the air smelt of spring freshness as well as autumnal decay. Wild flowers drooped at the end of their season. A pair of squirrels were foraging for food or perhaps burying winter rations close to the roots of a tree.

A mile down the track they came to a shallow pond, fed by a spring which bubbled a gentle turbulence in the centre. One end of the pond rippled into a me-andering stream. A frog vaulted into the water at their approach, secreting itself under a fringe of watercress.

With a cavalier flourish Andrew threw his raincoat over a sunlit patch of moss and fallen leaves and they sat down. It was a mild afternoon, almost warm in the shelter of the forest which faintly rustled and creaked around them. Evelyn shrugged off her mink and kicked off her shoes and galoshes. 'This is pretty,' she con-ceded, lying back on her coat and his.

Andrew kept his shoes clear of the coat. 'An oasis of tranquillity,' he said. She ignored the irony in his tone.

'Yes,' she said and yawned.

'Sorry if I'm boring you.'

'It's not you, idiot. I'm a bit tired. All that driving.'

'And the stress. Cuba. Pilgrim. Me.'

'You can be maddening sometimes' – she smiled, infected by his teasing – 'but you're not stressful.'

'Look, if you want to snooze, I don't mind.'

'I'll just close my eyes for a couple of minutes,' she said and did so. The silence of the wood was intimi-dating; she opened her eyes, saw Andrew, smiled at him again, then closed her eyes once more and fell instantly asleep.

THE SOUND OF splashing awoke her some twenty minutes later. She opened her eyes and sat up. He was paddling in the pond. As well as taking off his shoes and socks he had removed his sweater and now wore only a string vest above his trousers rolled up to the knees. It was so untypical of Andrew that she burst out laughing.

He grinned. 'Come on in, the water's lovely!'

'It looks freezing,' she said, still laughing at him.

'Well, it's not a thermal spring, but the mud feels very therapeutic.'

'An open-air mud bath – no thanks! Anyway, I've got stockings on.'

'Take them off. Live dangerously for once. I won't look.' He made a performance of turning his back.

'I've lived dangerously enough for one week,' she said. But she rolled down her stockings and tucked them into a pocket of her coat. Andrew turned and offered her both his hands, and she stepped off the bank. The water was shockingly, achingly, cold. Evelyn gasped, but with another mocking smile he held on to her hands and drew her into the middle. Beneath their feet the mud faintly pulsed.

'Isn't that invigorating?' he insisted.

'It's certainly unusual,' she allowed, 'but my feet are going numb.' She freed her hands and made her own way out of the pool, Andrew following.

'How do we get dry?' she asked.

'We just let nature take its course,' he replied. They lay down side by side on the two coats, in the sun-shine. Leaning over her on his elbow, he kissed her briefly, almost casually it seemed, on the lips. Evelyn felt her face burning and hoped it was from the sun and not a schoolgirl blush. After Thursday even a kiss should feel like a violation, she knew, but it hadn't.

'What's that in aid of?' she asked with a smile.

'Does it have to be in aid of something?' His lightly tanned face still loomed over hers. She could smell his cologne which was lemony. His blue-grey eyes held a hint of challenge, of mockery. The sun haloed his dark-brown hair.

'Andrew, you dye your hair!' She came out with this before she could stop herself. He laughed.

'Oh dear, are my roots showing? I swear this is positively the *last* of my secrets.'

'Well, I have mine highlighted,' she confessed.

'Evelyn.'

'What?'

'I've told you before: you have no sense of occasion.'

'Why, what's the occasion today?'

'Shut up,' he said, almost crossly, and kissed her again, a tender but longer kiss. When he ended it she put her arms round his neck, drew his head down and brought his mouth back onto hers. Disordered thoughts flooded her mind: Pilgrim, the kitchen, Sidney, home, Cuba; she pushed them away. Her heart was pounding: she willed it to slow its beat.

'Andrew, I –' she began, freeing her mouth.

'Don't speak,' he reminded her. She surrendered to him, closing her eyes as he kissed them lightly. He kissed her eyes, her chin, her neck. Evelyn was faintly aware of his fingers deftly unbuttoning her jacket and removing it, removing her blouse, unfastening and removing her bra; and then she felt his mouth, his tongue, on her breasts. Her nipples began to throb, almost painfully, an unfamiliar sensation. His hands remained deft and busy and she became momentarily aware of the air, the weak sun, on her lower body before this awareness was overtaken by the sensation of his hands, now here, now there. There was a corner of her mind that told her she was being raped for a second time, but whatever this was – and it was clearly wrong in so many ways – it didn't feel like rape.

He was gone from her a moment and when he returned he was naked: she felt his warm skin, the hair on his chest, his hardness against her and, again, his hands, his mouth. And then he parted – or she parted – her thighs and he lifted her – she raised herself – to meet him, and the hardness slid inside her; and still she felt his fingers and his mouth on her; and the sliding continued, and there began in Evelyn another new sensation, both exquisite and alarming, rapidly overwhelming her: a sensation that was flaring and rushing and heaving and flooding altogether. *This is it*, she thought, *this is how it's meant to be*, and there came into her mind an image not of the man who'd been making love to her for fifteen years without making this happen, but of the one, dead for twenty years who'd never had the chance to do this to her. *Tony*, she said his name in her mind, feeling sad and happy and bitter all at once; and then the strange new sensations built to a sudden crescendo and she cried out and she thought that Andrew too said something that was drowned by her own cry; and then, just as suddenly, it was over.

A bird – a thrush – chirruped overhead. Evelyn also heard the rustling of the stream that ran out of the pond and the thudding of her heartbeat as it slowly returned to normal. She could hardly believe that Andrew's tender romantic touch had allowed her to surrender so easily to something she'd expected to fill her with nausea after – Thursday. She turned her head to look at him, sprawled now alongside her on the crumpled coats, as naked as she was, his hair mussed where she must have clung to it during their passion, his eyes closed, his mouth smeared with her lipstick and moist with saliva, the hair on his chest matted with perspiration, his organ slick and wilting like one of the wild flowers. He opened his eyes and smiled his familiar mocking smile.

'Well, look at you, Lady C. – or may I call you Constance?'

'No teasing, Andrew – please.'

'Evelyn, you came.'

'And I'm glad I did,' she said. 'If I'd stayed in London or gone to Holland –'

'Darling Evelyn – is it OK if I call you darling now? – I don't mean you came. I mean, you *came*.' He re-emphasized the last word. 'Either that or you've been faking brilliantly all these years with Sid.'

Another vision came into Evelyn's mind, still not of the husband she had now cuckolded for the second time in forty-eight hours, but of her long-dead mother, an amiable countrywoman who took her churchgoing seriously and had hung the parlour walls of their farmhouse with all ten Commandments, crocheted with unfussy but devoted stitch-work. The injunction against Adultery dominated the fireplace wall, its prominence directed at Father, a meek man with no aspirations in that (or any other) direction. A decade had elapsed since Evelyn had last entered a church (for her mother's funeral) other than as a sightseer, but the reverberating texts of her Devonshire childhood still struck uneasy, guilty chords.

'Let's not talk about Sid,' she said.

Along with this second vision there came sounds: a horse whinnied; a dog barked. The vision was in Evelyn's guilty mind, but the sounds were real and not far off. 'I think we've no longer got the wood to ourselves,' Andrew said. 'It might be a good idea to put our clothes on.'

They dressed, Andrew unhurriedly, Evelyn with frantic haste as she imagined being, like the woman in St John's Gospel – literally – '*taken in adultery*'.

A man on horseback rode into the clearing beside the pond. Both he and his mount were old and shabby. An Alsatian that was little more than a puppy scampered into the clearing behind them and barked at the down-from-the-city strangers, the woman in an expensive fur coat applying lipstick and the younger man in a long raincoat to which leaves clung.

'Hush now, Scamp,' the man said to the dog and then, addressing Andrew and Evelyn: 'Lovely day, b'ain't it?' He had a broad Sussex accent which lengthened these short phrases.

'It certainly is,' Andrew acknowledged with a grin at Evelyn. He bent down and offered a hand to the puppy who approached it cautiously. Evelyn, concentrating on the ever more mysterious reflection in her make-up mirror, mustered a smile for the old yokel.

THEY WALKED IN silence through the once more silent wood. He took her arm as they navigated a large puddle and they stayed arm-in-arm until they were back at the car. He kissed her hands and released her with another challenging smile. While Evelyn put her galoshes in a plastic bag in the boot, Andrew wiped his Florentine shoes as clean as he could on clumps of grass and moss.

'Where do we go from here?' he asked as she reversed cautiously across the puddled ruts.

'Another nice tea-shop?' she suggested.

He smiled. 'I meant *us*. Where do *we* go from here?' The car skidded as she engaged first gear and pointed it back down the lane.

'I can't think about that while I'm driving,' she prevaricated, although this and related thoughts were making it difficult to concentrate on the car's slithering progress. And something – a leaf, a twig, pondweed? – was scratching between two of her toes.

BEFORE LUNCHTIME LAURENCE had resolved the 'demarcation' dispute between the Housekeeper and the Senior Room Service Steward (both threatening resignation) that had brought him to Brighton. The Manager could have settled it, but allowing the Owner to arbitrate enabled the Manager to maintain his seeming impartiality.

This was the largest of Laurence's five hotels (at fifty bedrooms twice the size of the one his grandfather had opened in Hastings), with his youngest and most dynamic manager. As the two men tucked into scallops and veal in the public restaurant, the Owner spared a thought for his wayward daughter, lunching in the staff dining room on soup and boiled haddock.

By mid-afternoon Laurence began to feel redundant. He waited by Reception where Sarah was registering two new arrivals. They had a sheepish air that was common among pre- and extra-marital fornicators. It was amazing how many of the great Smith clan weekended in Brighton. Laurence would have liked to thank this pair. Their illicit incontinence was going to help fund his proposed expansion onto the Continent.

'Do enjoy your stay, Mr and Mrs – er – Smith,' his daughter said as she handed them their key. 'Have you come to rescue me from this four-star brothel of yours?' she asked her father, within earshot of the er-Smiths.

'This brothel put you through Benenden,' he reminded her.

'HAVE I HELPED YOU?' Evelyn asked.

'Helped me what?'

'Helped you – back on the straight and narrow. After – you know – *him*.' She couldn't bring herself to say his name, but the vile thing that he'd made her do seemed further than forty-eight hours in the past.

He laughed. 'Darling, I rather think you helped yourself.' Her face clouded.

'Don't be mean,' she said. The sky too had clouded over since they left the wood; rain now pattered down the leaded windows of the tea-shop next to his grandmother's former home in Mayfield. Across the small Victorian table Andrew took her hand, eliciting narrow glances from two narrow spinsters who were the only other customers.

'Sorry, darling, I'm teasing you again. I think we've both helped each other get over – recent occurrences. It was very nice.' He smiled at her with unaffected sincerity and wished he'd come up with a stronger endorsement.

Evelyn's eyes brimmed with tears. 'It was' – she also had to search for words and managed to come up with – 'lovely.' She freed her hand and fumbled in her coat pocket for her handkerchief. Her stockings came momentarily into view, but she stuffed them back down before the hawk-eyed biddies across the room could glimpse them and confirm their most ambitious expect-ations. Evelyn wiped her eyes. 'I'm never going to forget it,' she added.

'Unforgettable' was a big improvement on both 'nice' and 'lovely', Andrew thought. 'We should have done it ages ago,' he said, trite when he needed to be grandiloquent.

'I don't know about that,' Evelyn replied quickly, too quickly. 'I was married in church. I made vows. Today I broke them.'

Andrew's sexual history since 1960 encompassed three other married women, each of whom had betray-ed her husband with vindictive relish. He slipped into his Noël Coward routine:

'My dear Evelyn, I've told you before, you really must try harder to shake off these bourgeois sen-sibilities.'

'I'm in no mood for your stupid impressions,' she retorted. Andrew tried not to look crushed.

'Sorry, darling,' he began carefully, 'but after fifteen years of being a faithful wife I really think you've *earned* what happened today.'

'Don't forget Torquay,' she said, lowering her voice to a near-whisper since the pair across the room were visibly straining to eavesdrop. After her threshing be-neath him in the wood not half an hour ago, Andrew felt piqued that Torquay came so speedily to her mind.

'*Almost* unfaithful doesn't count,' he said quietly.

'And – Pilgrim.' There: she *could* name him.

'Against your will doesn't count either.' He reached for her hand again but Evelyn, increasingly aware of the silent witnesses across the room, removed both hands to her lap where they anxiously twisted her handkerchief.

'It's this end-of-the-world feeling,' she said. 'In a normal week none of this would have happened. Maybe that woman in the pub was right. The old prophecies are coming true. Strange things are happening all over – not just in Cuba.'

Andrew checked her expression; she seemed to be serious. 'You think our Pilgrim might be' – his tone became sepulchral – '"not of this world"?'

Evelyn nodded at what she apparently saw as his sagacity. 'Why does he keep disappearing? Where are they now? Did he really go to Dover yesterday, or to Walthamstow on Thursday?'

'Wasn't it Hammersmith on Thursday? That's what he told Laurence.'

'Walthamstow, he told me,' she insisted. 'One of Sid's craftsmen lives there.'

'Oh well, Laurence may have misheard. Or maybe Pilgrim told you both a different fib.'

'Maybe he goes all over the place ruining people's lives. Not just ours.'

Andrew could hardly believe they were having this conversation. 'And how does Malcolm fit in? I agree Pilgrim's a very creepy individual, but the boy seems completely harmless.'

'Perhaps he's some sort of *disciple*.'

'What, like a witch with her black cat? A – what's the word? – a "familiar"?' Evelyn nodded sagely again. 'Well, if Pilgrim *is* the *Antichrist* or' – he struggled to keep a straight face – 'one of the Horsemen of the Apocalypse that madwoman was prophesying, it's very modern of them to be using motorbikes!' Evelyn still did not smile. 'Which of the Horsemen could he be?'

Andrew wondered aloud. 'I imagine Pestilence has a fairly large remit. Come to think of it' – it surprised him that he could turn his 'ordeal' on the sofa into a joke – 'I did catch a whiff of *brimstone* from him yesterday.' His straight face cracked and he laughed.

She rounded on him. 'I suppose you think I'm being as ridiculous as that woman.' She forced herself to laugh. 'I *am* being ridiculous. This is what he's done to me.'

I thought I'd fucked some sense into you, Andrew would have liked to say. He tried to convey this without being brutal, keeping his voice low. 'Evelyn – dearest Evelyn – forget that bloody woman and her lunatic notions. I agree we've had an unusual week, but what we did today has nothing to do with Pilgrim or with what's happening in Cuba. The earth finally moved for you, but it wasn't Armageddon, it was an *orgasm!*'

The buxom proprietress, whose nose was raw and red from a streaming cold, chose this moment to arrive at their table with a laden tray. Since she didn't drop two Sussex Cream Teas onto the bare floorboards, Andrew inferred that she hadn't heard – or was unfamiliar with – his last word. Evelyn made neither of these assumptions. Her whole face went the colour of the proprietress's alarming proboscis. Across the room the two old maids exchanged knowing looks.

HAVING HEARD THE car pull up, the housekeeper bustled into the hall from the corridor to the kitchen as Laurence and Sarah came through the front door.

'Your wife has phoned twice today, Mr Dickinson.'

'No such person exists, Mrs Danvers,' he retorted, winking at Sarah.

'Your former wife,' conceded the housekeeper, to whom 'ex-wife' smacked of the music hall. *Mr* Ormsby-Lowndes, who had run off with a fan dancer from London's Windmill Theatre, was not referred to as her 'ex-husband'. He was rarely referred to at all. Mrs Ormsby-Lowndes had not descended into domestic service during Laurence's marriage and had only met the former Mrs Dickinson in 1960 when she visited her first husband and their sixteen-year-old daughter following the death of Luigi the Perfume Prince. Mercifully, it had been a short visit. Louise had had other fish to fry or, rather, to *net*, in the matrimonial sea.

'And what did Her Highness my mother have to say?' Sarah enquired, joining in the game. Mrs Danvers sniffed, a sniff that said 'your mother that barmaid.'

'She said she would call again.'

'I must arrange to be out,' said Laurence.

'It was Miss Sarah she was most anxious to speak to.'

Sarah made a face. 'I'm going to be permanently out too.'

'Is Andrew here?' Laurence asked. Mrs Danvers' grey hair was scraped into a tighter-than-usual bun; not a hair shivered as she shook her head.

'Mrs Hunter returned in the middle of the morning. They went out for lunch but promised to be back in time for this evening's – celebration.'

'Did Andrew speak to Sarah's mother?' Laurence smiled at this tempting but unlikely prospect. Andrew had been summoned from London in 1960 to meet Louise in her widow's weeds, which although strenuously black bore ostentatiously Roman hallmarks. Over her hair – still a vibrant titian but more subtly styled than it had been in Hastings – she was sporting a confection of black lace and diamanté (or possibly *diamonds*). Andrew greeted this spectacle with something between a curtsy and a bow. 'Your Highness, such an honour – and how splendid to find you in such rude grief.'

'Is he a fairy?' demanded Louise who'd evidently been keeping company with Americans in Rome. 'He talks like a fairy.'

A twitch in the creases surrounding her pursed lips suggested that Mrs Danvers was also remembering this meeting. 'It was one o'clock when she called. He'd already left with Mrs Hunter.'

'That's five a.m. in California,' Sarah calculated. 'A late night even for Mother.'

'She's not in America,' Mrs Danvers informed them with an expression appropriate to the delivery of mixed tidings. 'She's in London. At Claridge's.'

'Dear God,' said Laurence.

'HAVE YOU EVER thought of living abroad?' Andrew asked, presumably just making conversation or trying to distract her.

'We've talked about it,' she replied. 'You know, when Sid retires. But we're more likely to go back to Devon. Or maybe Cornwall.'

'Not very adventurous.'

She smiled at him. 'Well, that's us: not very adventurous. Not like you.' She wound her window shut as a gust of wind rocked the car and blew raindrops through the gap. The shower had become a downpour. Straddling the Greenwich Meridian, they were parked in the grounds of Herstmonceux Castle; its cluster of observatory domes rose from the downland like a tray of buns. Evelyn wondered if it was their promise of the furthest reaches of exploration that had prompted his question.

'I've been toying with the idea of going abroad to live,' he said.

'Have you? Lucky you!' *We're talking as if we've just been introduced,* she thought. *How do you do, my husband's a jeweller in Bond Street, we live in Hampstead Garden Suburb. Really? I have a business in*

Mayfair, but I'm moving to – 'Where do you think you'll go?' she asked.

'I haven't exactly made up my mind.' The wind plastered some leaves onto the windscreen. 'I thought of Italy or Spain, but it might be somewhere a bit further off the track. Morocco, for instance.'

Evelyn immediately thought of sand and scorpions; she shivered. As they waited out the rainstorm, he spoke of his travels in Morocco: from the green mountains of the Rif to the pink granite of the Atlas; gorges and cataracts; oases and fortresses on the edge of the Sahara; palaces, mosques, medinas and souks. The atmosphere inside the car became misty and muggy not from English rain and cigarette smoke but from desert humidity and the smoke rising from village campfires.

'I can't imagine living in a country like that,' Evelyn said. The Hunters took safe prosaic holidays. And yet she felt, faintly, the attraction of a destination where the foetid spicy air carried also a whiff of danger.

'Come wiz me to ze casbah,' Andrew said in the accent of Maurice Chevalier, forgetting her injunction against his impersonations and twirling an imaginary moustache at her. Evelyn had forgotten too: she laughed. 'I mean it,' he said.

'You mean ...'

'Leave Sidney and come with me.' Evelyn blanched as a few words turned her life upside down. 'It needn't be Morocco,' he added. 'It can be Paris or Rome or Madrid.' His eyes scorched her like the Saharan sun. 'It could just be South Kensington.'

Evelyn felt helpless, torn, divided, and ultimately hopeless. She was still conscious of the hovering shadow of her mother, wagging a finger as she had been wont to do to remind her daughter of some neglected chore: room not tidied, homework unfinished, chickens unfed. Never one to mince her words, Mother would have had a few Biblical epithets to describe a woman who contemplated leaving her husband for another man, a man twelve years her junior.

'Andrew, you know I can't up and leave Sid just like that,' she said, fighting back tears.

His eyes challenged hers as they so often did, but they no longer mocked. 'Yes you can, Evelyn. Just like that. If it's what you want.'

'I don't know what I want,' she said. 'Maybe I never have. I just – drift.' *How pathetic I sound*, she thought. She also thought that there must be millions of people who went through life that same way: drifting.

'Come and drift with me,' he said, as if it were that simple. It couldn't be that simple. She stared through the windscreen. The rain was lessening as the dark clouds swept towards the coast, to the Channel and on to – who knew? – Paris and Rome or Madrid. She looked at him again.

'I'm twelve years older than you,' she reminded him, as her mother had – from beyond the grave – somehow just managed to remind her.

'What's that got do with anything?'

'You can't expect me to leave my husband just to become one more mare in your stable.'

'That's not what I'm asking. I'm not inviting you to become my mistress. I'm asking you to divorce Sidney and marry me.'

So simple, again. But she almost laughed. 'I can't imagine you married.' He conceded the point with another smile.

'Try to imagine me married to you.'

She did laugh, weakly, defensively. 'I can't.'

'You can't imagine it or you think you can't marry me?'

'Either. Both.' What he was saying, what he had done to her in the woods, had driven Pilgrim and what *he'd* done out of the foreground of her consciousness, but she was still aware of him hovering in a distant corner; and behind Pilgrim there still loomed the mushroom clouds threatened by Kennedy and Krushchev.

'Think about it some more,' he said. 'Let's get going. The rain's stopped. We're going to need baths before dinner.'

As Evelyn started the engine, another car pulled into the parking area, driven by an angry-looking man with a younger woman, a blonde who might have been pretty but for the misery stamped on her features. Was she a browbeaten wife, Evelyn wondered; or another guilt-racked Jezebel?

'MR DICKINSON?' THE kind of well-bred switchboard operator a top hotel would employ. Laurence's heart sank. He should have let Mrs Danvers answer the phone.

'Yes,' he confessed.

'I have a call for you.' Before she could get off the line a familiar strident voice was demanding: 'Larry? Is that you, Larry honey?'

'Louise,' Laurence said with an unexpurgated sigh. 'What brings you to these shores?'

'You maht sound a bit more pleased to hear me,' she drawled. 'An' you can hardly expect me to stay over there when that crazy Catholic in the Whaht House is tryin' to get us all blown to Hayel.'

His ex-wife's accent was like the Bexhill Dramatic Society's least leading lady auditioning for *Showboat*. Laurence managed to censor a second sigh. 'Of course not, Louise. Have you brought the entire Republican Party with you?'

Her good-natured cackle almost ruptured the diaphragm of his earpiece. Laurence moved the phone a short distance from his head. 'Still the same old Larry,' she said. 'Still full of the same old shit. No, hon, there's just me and Howard, the man with whom I've just gotten engaged to.' Laurence memorized her prepositions to repeat to Andrew. 'And we brought Howie Junior, of course.'

'Well, you could hardly leave little Howie to the mercy of those frightful Democrats,' Laurence said, fighting a rising sense of confusion. Sarah appeared in the doorway and grimaced at Laurence who replied with a comical screwing-up of his own face. 'You're at Claridge's, aren't you? I suppose you want Sarah to come up and see you.' His daughter threatened him with the tennis racket she'd left in the hall.

'Or we could come and visit with you-all.'

'Not this week, Louise,' he said quickly. 'I've got guests. Including Andrew.' This would head her off, he thought. It did.

'That faggot,' she spat. 'I don't like the idea of him hangin' round my precious little girl.'

'Your precious little girl handles herself pretty well,' he said more dourly than he intended. Sarah frowned. 'She's learning the hotel trade,' he went on, 'so I shan't be able to spare her for more than a day or two.' Sarah forgave him with a smile.

'Well, I was hopin' she could come back with us for our weddin' next month. We're getting' married in Hawaii.'

'I don't know how Sarah will feel about Hawaii.' Sarah's expression put Hawaii – in her mother's company – on a par with the Bexhill branch of Moral Rearmament.

'Is Sarah there? Put her on.'

'No, you've just missed her. She's – gone to the tennis club.' His daughter blew him a grateful kiss. He heard footsteps in the hall and the sound of the front door closing. 'Louise, I have to go. My guests are here. I'll have Sarah get back to you tomorrow.' His ex-wife drew breath for another raucous protest. Laurence quickly hung up and followed Sarah through the doorway into the hall where Mrs Danvers was helping Evelyn off with her coat.

'Evelyn,' Laurence said. 'I'm so glad you came back to us. And how well you look. Our country air's given you a real *glow*.' Evelyn's 'glow' deepened.

'I just got off the phone to Louise,' Laurence told Andrew. 'You'll be thrilled to hear –' The doorbell rang. He broke off and moved to reopen the front door. A taxi had pulled up behind Evelyn's Renault. Its driver stood at the top of the steps, his broad body shielding the figure of his passenger who held a modest leather suitcase. The driver tipped his cap at Laurence.

'Evenin', sir,' he said in a rich Kentish burr. 'I've brought this gentleman all the way from Dover, but he says he hasn't got the money to pay me.'

He stepped aside to reveal his passenger who also raised his hat, a ludicrous English trilby, as he mounted the top step.

'Carlo!' Laurence exclaimed in amazement. The new arrival smiled, exposing film-star teeth in his tanned film-star face.

'Signor Lorenzo.'

Behind Laurence Sarah dropped her tennis racket.

'*Sharlz!*' she gasped.

Andrew had just handed the housekeeper his rumpled raincoat. He bent down and picked up the racket.

'Mixed doubles, anyone?' he enquired with a cheerful laugh.

IN WASHINGTON AND Cuba it was still morning as the crisis reached its third 'flashpoint' and claimed its first (and only) casualty. A U-2 reconnaissance plane was shot down by a surface-to-air missile over Cuba, killing its pilot, Air Force Major Rudolf Anderson Jr., one of the two pilots who had brought the first photographs of the suspect installations.

At the White House the 'hawks' were in the ascendant. The Joint Chiefs of Staff had just submitted to the President their recommendation of military action in place of the blockade: an air strike against the missile sites, to be followed by an air-and-sea invasion of Cuba. They were discussing the 'nuclear option' when the news came of the downed plane.

EVENING

LAURENCE HAD ARRANGED a cocktail party for Andrew and Evelyn's last evening. Aware that the doyens and dowagers of what passed for 'society' in Bexhill would provide a meagre audience for Andrew's urbane repartee (and might not be amused), he'd invited a half-dozen younger couples from the tennis club and some of his less stuffy neighbours.

'Shall I add the junior Yateses to the guest list, or would that add insult to yesterday's rude injury?' he had asked Andrew this morning, taking a cup of tea up to his room before setting out for Brighton.

Andrew pondered for only a moment before replying: 'Yes, go on: why not. Let's see how I feel about David now that I've been re-inducted into the world of rough manly sex.'

Offered dinner as well as drinks, David said that he would be glad to come, but his wife didn't feel well enough to go out. Ruth had already been invited as company for Sarah, not that Sarah set much store by Ruth's company. As a 'surprise' for Andrew Laurence also called an ex-colleague of his from Plummer Roddis, the Hastings department store: Graham Collins was a leading light of two drama groups and the operatic society. A year or two older than Andrew, he walked with a mincing gait and accompanied his speech with flapping hand gestures. On the Kings Road in Chelsea Andrew had once introduced Laurence to an acquaintance with purple bouffant hair, wearing a silk trouser-suit, high-heeled shoes, a chiffon cravat and a noticeable quantity of make-up. Graham Collins, at a significantly lower pitch, was Bexhill's answer to Quentin Crisp. He could be counted on to be the 'life and soul' of any party he attended, and he was free this evening.

'Sweetie,' he said, 'in Bexhill I'm always free on Saturdays and extremely reasonable on weekdays and Sundays!' Laurence wondered if there was some kind of Camp School that Andrew and Graham had both graduated from, they spoke with such similar intonation, Graham all the time, Andrew only when he wanted to affect it. 'But I'll take a rain check on dinner, if you'll excuse me. I have a "gentleman caller" on Sundays and I need an early night before so much rigorous activity. You can boot me out with the tennis club winos.'

Those not staying for dinner would leave after seventy-five to ninety minutes. Bexhill cocktail parties adhered to a rigid format.

It was fortunate that Laurence had asked the cook to prepare something substantial, now that they again had extra mouths to feed. She was already plying the latest arrival with tea and cake as Laurence went up to change for dinner.

He felt tense and apprehensive. Evelyn seemed to be all right, but was she? Andrew was joking about Pilgrim's assault, but was he really undamaged by it? And what, in God's name, was he going to do about Sarah and Carlo?

Knotting his bow tie at the window overlooking the terrace, Laurence sighed.

ANDREW, IN HIS attic, was also on edge. Literally so, it
seemed.

The view he'd affected in the teashop to accom-
modate Evelyn's apparent hysteria over Pilgrim had
been nothing more than an elaborate tease. *Preter-
natural Pilgrim*, the 'motorcycling demon', and Malcolm
the mute 'acolyte' – it was all so blatantly preposterous
that it rather shocked him that she'd given the notion
even passing credence in the guilty aftermath of their
woodland 'shag'. Pilgrim was surely nothing more sinister than a rampaging sexual opportunist, a 'cuckoo'
fouling every nest that he chanced upon? And maybe
Malcolm was less innocent than he looked, not just a
pillion passenger but along for the occasional *sexual*
ride.

There was no denying that yesterday's experience
in the music room had brought Andrew to some sort of
brink. On one side stood Evelyn and the chance she
now offered of a conventional, 'normal' life. On the
other stood Laurence, too timid to do more than peer
yearningly across the threshold of the homosexual
world; Laurence who, once Sarah flew the nest with
one of her Tennis Club 'oiks', might degenerate into a
loneliness like Algie's. Algie represented everything
that Andrew dreaded becoming: a man defeated by
life, his talent burnt-out, a sour and seedy middle-aged
queen awash with booze and bitterness.

He could not, he knew, go back to the charade of
his affairs with Fiona and others of the Sloane Square
set. That way lay another kind of dead-end. He had not
expected this, but suddenly everything depended on
Evelyn. Would she go with him, or would she cast him
back into that metaphorical chasm?

Shrugging on his dinner jacket in the Moorish –
Moroccan! – attic, Andrew sighed, then smiled to
himself. Today – tomorrow – seemed to be offering a
dramatic range of choices: matrimony, promiscuity or

Armageddon!

EVELYN PUT TO one side the immense decision Andrew had presented her with and concentrated on the
more mundane but immediate one of what to wear for
dinner.

Already indecisive this morning, she had packed
two contrasting dresses for her last evening. Both were
calf-length. One was lilac-and-grey layered tulle over a
grey silk bodice and underskirt, hardly suitable for October if they dined out, but surely perfect for Bexhill's
grey-haired and lilac-rinsed geriatric set. The other was
a more daring red silk.

The silk was two years old, but Andrew had not
seen her in it. The tulle was new, bought last week. It
had cost 85 guineas, probably what the South Molton
Street seamstress who altered it to fit Evelyn earned in
three months or the shop's elegant French manager-
ess in six weeks. Sidney could make 85 guineas in
profit on a single 'mid-range' engagement ring assem-
bled from the gleanings of one of his Dutch trips.
Evelyn would wear the dress a maximum of five or six
times.

Looking at both dresses now, she sighed. Really
the tulle was a bit drab, almost dowdy. That French-
man or Italian or whatever he was – she could hear
him showering in the bathroom across the landing –
would probably still be wearing the crumpled brown
suit in which he'd arrived. She hung the tulle back
inside her wardrobe and put on the silk. *A scarlet
dress*, she thought with a smile that was a little grim
and more than a little guilty, *for a 'scarlet woman'*. Stop
haunting me, Mother.

SARAH, IN HER bath, sighed with anticipation as she
soaped between her thighs, pressing the bar of lemon-
scented soap against her mound, almost pushing it into

her cleft which throbbed with an anticipation of its own. '*Sharlz*', she thought. His name, the thought of him – and what she was doing with the soap – brought her to the nerve-tingling brink of orgasm.

He would be hers tonight! He would take her to – there had to be a sexual place that was beyond merely 'going all the way'.

And then, next month, perhaps she *would* go to Hawaii for her mother's fifth wedding. American men were surely worth trying? Imagine doing it with a man like George Maharis or Ty Hardin! She pressed harder with the soap and bit her lip to keep herself from crying aloud.

IN THE DRAWING ROOM Laurence handed Andrew a gin-and-tonic. They clinked glasses.

'Here's to the latest addition to your staff,' Andrew said. 'He's certainly quite a bit prettier than Mrs Danvers!'

Laurence laughed. 'Didn't I say he was devastating?' His expression turned sour. 'I never expected that my new chauffeur would turn out to be Sarah's lost summer romance. I pictured her "Sharlz" as one of those scruffy student types, vaguely intellectual-looking, perhaps with glasses and a few spots.'

'How come you never saw a photo of him?'

'She didn't take a camera to London with her.' He put his glass down. 'She told me the other day that she's still a virgin,' he went on uneasily, 'but how long's that going to be the case – assuming it's even true?'

Andrew continued to smile. 'Well, given her admitted weakness for the back seat of cars, you'll have to make sure Carlo only chauffeurs *you* and not her.'

'Andrew, that isn't funny.' He sighed. 'Well, I shall encourage Louise to whisk her off to Hawaii and while she's away I can send Carlo packing.'

'After at least sampling the goods, I hope.' Andrew

arched his eyebrows. Laurence turned on him.

'Is that what everything comes down to with you: sex, sex, sex?'

'Don't get hoity-toity with me, "Signor Lorenzo". You didn't invite him here to discuss Giotto's frescoes. Let's face it, you didn't really invite him here to drive your car.'

Laurence admitted defeat with a rueful smile. 'I don't know what possessed me. Yes, I do. I told you the other day: he reminded me of you. Seeing him again today, the resemblance is stronger than I realized. He's got your height, your build, your looks, even your hair.'

Andrew laughed again, enjoying the comparison. 'Aside from the fact that my hair's dyed a few shades darker than its natural colour, I feel like a very rough draft of what turned out to be your Carlo. Besides which, isn't it time you looked for a different model? You haven't had a lot of luck with this one.'

Laurence coloured. 'You're right, of course.' The door opened. In the hall the doorbell rang again. It was six twenty-eight. The first arrivals were two minutes early. Evelyn entered the drawing room.

'The Lady in Red!' Andrew exclaimed.

HAVING WITNESSED EVELYN'S and Mrs Danvers' reaction to the Cuban crisis, Laurence was expecting a few cancellations and no-shows. But by six forty-two everybody had come.

As if by a silent consensus, the crisis was not discussed. People made the usual small talk: tennis, golf, bridge, local affairs, the cost of living, the weather, cars. Predictably, the tennis club people mainly spoke to each other and to Sarah and Ruth; the neighbours formed another clique. Mrs Danvers circulated with miniature sandwiches and sausage rolls, Carlo and Laurence with trays of wine glasses. Like Laurence and Andrew, Carlo wore a dinner jacket, although his was badly creased and had clearly seen service during his career as a waiter. Andrew circulated with Evelyn on his arm, equally at ease with the people he'd met before and those he hadn't. He and Graham greeted each other with Continental kisses on the cheek. Graham was dressed for a production of *The Boy Friend*: a red-striped cotton jacket, a cerulean-blue shirt, white flannel trousers, brown-and-white 'co-respondent' shoes.

'Evelyn, this is Graham. Who also answers to the name of Gloria.'

Evelyn looked more puzzled than surprised.

'Gloria Grahame,' the debonair young man explained. 'You know: "I'm Just a Girl Who Cain't Say No".' He all but sang the title.

'It's as true of this one as it was of the screen Gloria,' Andrew added.

'Ooh, there's the pot calling the kettle a blackened tart,' Graham said, his voice rising an octave. Evelyn perceived that the world of men like Graham and Andrew was like – perhaps actually *was* – the world of Sandy Wilson musicals. She wondered if Graham had been Andrew's – what was the word? – 'boyfriend'?

Apart from these two, gliding around the drawing room like the Redcoats at a Butlins holiday camp (not that Evelyn had ever been to one), the cocktail party was almost unreal in its nonchalant normality. But then today – this week – had redefined everything that passed for normal in her life.

One of the tennis club wives smiled at Evelyn. 'Your dress is divine. Where did you get it?'

Evelyn smiled back. 'In Bond Street.'

'That street with funny little shops in Brighton?'

Evelyn shook her head. 'The one with funny big shops in London.'

She looked for Andrew to rescue her. No sooner

had she registered his absence than the sound of the piano came from the opened doors of the adjoining music room, followed by a pleasing light tenor voice singing 'Someday My Heart Will Awake'. Evelyn went in and sat in the chair at which she'd played whist with Laurence two nights ago, some three hours before she went to the kitchen and found Pilgrim peering into the fridge. All but two of the neighbours and half of the tennis set followed her into the music room.

'SHARLZ, I'VE GOT to talk to you.'

'Sara' – as he had last year in London, Carlo spoke her name with Continental vowels, although his accent was less pronounced than she remembered – 'I cannot talk now. I have to look after the drinks for these people.'

'They can help themselves. They usually do. Let's go somewhere and *talk*.'

'Your father asked me to come here to work. He gave me money for my train ticket.'

'But you're only here to drive his car.'

'Tonight he asked me to help with the drinks. We can talk later – or tomorrow.'

EVELYN LED THE applause when the Novello song finished. Graham then sang 'If Ever I Would Leave You' from *Camelot*, a show which had not yet come to London (Andrew had given Evelyn the LP of the New York production). Staying on Broadway, Graham launched into a raucous Ethel Merman impersonation with 'The Hostess With the Mostess'. In the same vein he sang the Elaine Stritch song 'Something Very Strange' from Noël Coward's *Sail Away*. Sidney and Evelyn had attended the show's first night at the Savoy Theatre in June with Andrew and his then girlfriend Jocelyn.

LAURENCE CAME IN from the drawing room during the
Elaine Stritch routine. He was grateful for the
impromptu entertainment, but his heart sank at the
thought that the pair might be tempted to perform a
composition of Andrew's called 'The Bexhill Beguine'
which they'd sung for him three years ago when
Andrew had been living here. Plagiarizing a Broadway
spoof of Cole Porter, Andrew had dashed it off in a
matter of minutes at the piano in the Methodist church
hall where the local amateur troupe rehearsed their
productions. It had some ribald verses which Laurence
preferred not to hear aired for the benefit of Evelyn and
the neighbours.

He too was finding the evening increasingly unreal.
Here they were drinking, chattering, listening to an
agreeably silly Noël Coward song like characters in
one of his plays, and on the other side of the Atlantic
decisions were being taken that would bring humanity
to the brink of catastrophe, extinction even. Was it 'the
Spirit of the Blitz'? Perhaps a party, some songs, a few
stiff drinks, was the best way to face the looming
apocalypse.

He was relieved when Graham went on to sing in
his normal voice another number from *Sail Away*,
'Later Than Spring', a song with much of the sugary
romance of Novello. After this, and very appropriate to
his outfit, he sang the title song from *The Boy Friend*,
affecting a shrill falsetto with much fluttering of his
hands and eyelashes. David, who had worn his tennis
club blazer and flannels, could have played a
supporting role at this point, but David and Ruth had
elected to stay in the drawing room. Andrew duetted
with Graham in 'I Could Be Happy With You' and then
'This Is My Lovely Day'. Graham had enough talent to
turn professional, Laurence thought, but Andrew's
singing, like his skill at the piano, was only that of a
gifted amateur. *Don't give up the day job, Andrew*, he

told him silently and smiled at the thought of how poorly this advice would be received.

EVELYN DIDN'T SEE a signal from Laurence but at the end of 'This Is My Lovely Day' Andrew took a bow and moved to join her on the other side of the piano. Graham joined one of the tennis club couples. Evelyn noticed that his attention drifted between Andrew and the Italian waiter.

'You two ought to do cabaret together,' she told Andrew.

'Actually, we're auditioning next month for the touring cast of *Sail Away*,' he told her straight-faced.

'Oh, but could Algie spare you from – you're teasing me, aren't you? But I do think your double act could make a nice sideline in nightclubs and party entertainment, like tonight. Graham would have to move to London. He could live with you – help with the rent.' She knew that Andrew lived permanently close to the edge of his means, if not beyond them.

'I think not. Gloria's a complete slut around the house. Her – his flat always looks as if it's been ransacked by burglars. He wouldn't fit in with my monastically austere surroundings. Besides which, I don't think you're quite ready for a *ménage à trois*, my love. Weren't we supposed to be making other plans?' His eyes challenged her.

She held up her hands as if to fend him off. 'Andrew, I – I can't make a decision about that. Not as quickly as – right now.'

'All right, darling. *Right now* we'd better go and help Laurence send these ghastly people packing.'

GRAHAM WAS GIVEN a lift home by the tennis club couple who'd brought him, Billy and Brenda. They'd seen him sing before, on the local stage and at other parties, but not with Andrew. In the car Brenda urged

Graham to take to the musical stage professionally. 'You'd have to go to London,' she told him, echoing Evelyn. 'But I don't see how you could fail – could he, Billy?'

'He'd be a smash success,' Billy said loyally, more loyal than his wife realized. The two men exchanged glances in the driving mirror. Both were perhaps thinking the same thing: that Brenda would be a lot keener to see Graham move to London if she knew that her husband was the 'gentleman caller' Graham had mentioned on the phone to Laurence. Almost every Sunday, while Brenda went to her favourite aunt's for tea, Billy, supposedly out taking a long healthy walk on the downs, spent two hours in Graham's first-floor flat on the seafront. Billy liked to dress up in women's clothing – costumes borrowed from the drama groups' wardrobes and a few frocks pilfered from the Hastings store where Graham worked – although Graham preferred Billy naked on top of his bed, face-up or face-down; Graham prided himself on his versatility.

Brenda's Aunt Glenys was one of Bexhill's many old maids. She shared a house in the Old Town with another spinster, a schoolteacher like herself. They lived a life of elaborate circumspection but, unknown to their neighbours as well as to both their families, they were a lesbian couple. They had lesbian friends in Brighton but not in Bexhill, although there were two other cohabiting pairs of spinsters in the town about whom they had their suspicions.

Bexhill was a bit less staid than Brenda and many of its citizens knew.

FOR DINNER LAURENCE sat in his usual chair at the head of the table nearest the fire, with Evelyn and Andrew in the pew on his right and David and Carlo on his left. Ruth and Sarah, in clashing frocks of green and blue, each occupied a whole pew on the bottom half of the table, Sarah making sure she got the one with the diagonal view of 'Sharlz'.

Evelyn ate little. Sarah fed her appetite on hungry looks in Carlo's direction. The object of her overheated attention looked exhausted but he ate heartily, as did Ruth and David; none of them spoke except when spoken to. Even Andrew seemed to find it burdensome tonight to keep the conversational ball rolling with such support as Laurence could muster. Cuba, to Laurence's relief, was not discussed.

The cocktail party food had served as a first course. Between the duck and the dessert Evelyn was summoned to the telephone.

'I just wanted to be sure you were back in Sussex,' her husband began.

'Where else would I have gone?'

'Well –' he chuckled, 'I wouldn't put it past Andrew to whisk you off to Paris or Florence or somewhere ... Hullo? Evelyn?'

'I'm still here.'

'I am too. I mean, I'm home. I decided not to bother with Rotterdam, so I came home instead. *You* don't need to come back any sooner ... When *are* you coming home, by the way ...? Hullo?'

'Tomorrow,' she said dully. 'Some time after lunch.'

'Are you all right? You sound a bit funny.'

'I'm fine. I'll see you tomorrow.'

'Night-night, dear.'

'Goodbye, Sid.'

MRS DANVERS BEGAN serving dessert as Evelyn resumed her place next to Andrew.

'So what's the news from Amsterdam?' he asked.

'He isn't in Amsterdam. He's come home a day early.'

'I hope this won't send you rushing off again,' said Laurence.

Evelyn avoided looking at Andrew. 'Not before to-morrow,' she said.

'Can *you* stay on a bit longer?' Laurence asked Andrew.

'No, I'll be leaving with Evelyn. Things to do, places to go. You know.' Evelyn continued to stare at her plate of summer pudding.

'I thought you could stay on and keep Carlo amused while Sarah goes to meet this latest poor chap with whom her mother's got engaged to.' Andrew acknowledged the second airing of Louise's prepositions with another smile.

'And Junior,' he contributed.

Sarah reluctantly diverted her gaze from their newest and handsomest guest. 'Who says I'm going to Mother?' she demanded.

'I do,' her father replied with menacing brevity.

'Then who's going to look after Sharlz?'

'Sara, you know I have come here to work for your father.'

'But I'm going to teach you tennis.'

'I already play tennis.'

'Well – you need to practise. You won't be working all the time. And neither will I,' she warned Laurence.

'*Some* work and *some* tennis,' he conceded.

'Among other games,' Andrew murmured.

'I STILL DON'T UNDERSTAND why you pretended to be French,' Sarah said in a low voice. Carlo was now seated beside her on a settee in the drawing room. David and Ruth sat on the other settee. Andrew and Evelyn stood at the window.

Carlo's tanned forehead furrowed. 'Sara, I was not pretending. I went to school in France. I have a French passport.'

'But you told my father you're Italian.'

'This is also the truth. I was born in Venice. My

father was Italian.'

'And why were you working as a waiter in Sitges? What happened to the professor you worked for last year?'

'She – he – was a writer, not a professor. I helped him with the research for one book. When we got back to Paris – he did not need me any more, so I went to Spain.'

'But why didn't you write to me?'

Carlo spread his hands in an expressive Italian gesture. Across the room Andrew caught his eye.

'Is she cross-examining you?' he called out. Sarah glared at him.

'I'm sorry?' said Carlo.

'*Elle vous interroge – Mamzelle le Gestapo.*' Carlo smiled broadly. Sarah flushed.

'Don't you dare call me the Gestapo.'

'Who's calling you the Gestapo?' asked her father, entering the room with the brandy decanter and glasses.

'Carlo's getting the third degree,' Andrew said.

'Give the poor fellow a rest,' Laurence told her. 'He's had a heavy couple of days.' He dispensed brandies to the adults and then sat on Carlo's other side.

'SO – ARE YOU planning to run back to Sid's ever-loving arms?' Andrew asked Evelyn quietly.

She continued to stare through the window, although there was little to see. The lights from the house illuminated the terrace and half of the lawn fading into the darkness of a cloudy night sky. 'What else can I do?'

'You know what else.'

She forced herself to look at him. 'Andrew, I've told you, I can't just – not go back.'

'But what would you be going back *for*? To do your duty? To honour vows you wish you hadn't made?'

'I've never said I wish I hadn't married Sid,' she protested.

'It's the truth though, isn't it?'

Evelyn was once again fighting back tears. 'Duty, honour,' she echoed. Those are the things that were drummed into me when I was small. At home and at school.'

'Into me too. I'll admit I'm a bit wobbly where honour is concerned, but I think duty has to include the duty to choose your own road through life.'

Evelyn was silent for a moment, digesting this. Then she said: 'I chose to walk with Sidney fifteen years ago.'

'And now I'm inviting you to walk with me instead.'

'Down the road to Morocco!' she said, trying to be humorous in the most serious situation she had ever faced. He smiled.

'I've told you: it doesn't have to be Morocco.'

'Morocco sounds wonderful,' she said, surprising herself as much as him.

'Are you two going to whisper into the curtains for the rest of the evening?' Laurence called from the sofa.

'Sorry,' said Andrew. 'We don't mean to be anti-social.' He drew Evelyn across the room to an armchair facing the two settees and sat on its arm.

For the next half-hour and with rather less effort than at dinner, Andrew dominated the conversation, comparing his Continental travels against Carlo's. Laurence managed to make a few contributions, and even David had some foreign holidays to mention. When Sarah joined in it was mostly with a question aimed at solving the riddle of Carlo's movements. Her eyes continued to devour him. Ruth listened with a show of interest, but Evelyn sat silently, plainly preoccupied and looking quite unhappy, Laurence thought. When he offered refills of their brandy glasses, Carlo excused himself to go to bed.

'Of course,' Laurence said. 'You must be shattered.'

'I'll take you upstairs,' Sarah offered.

'He knows the way to his room, for God's sake,' said Laurence. 'No, on second thoughts: you can go to your room. Take Ruth with you. Play some records, but keep the sound down. And leave Carlo in peace, at least till tomorrow.'

Sarah pouted at being, once again, banished like a child, but she did not miss the chance to scoot after Carlo, Ruth keenly following.

UNFORTUNATELY FOR BOTH girls, with a yawned 'Goodnight, Sara; goodnight, *signorina*' (he'd forgotten Ruth's name), Carlo went into the room that had been Malcolm's and closed the door behind him.

'He's incredibly gorgeous, isn't he?' Ruth lisped even before they got to Sarah's rooms. 'Did you ever – you know' – a blush highlighted her pimples – 'with him, like you did with that motorbike chap?'

'Oh yes,' Sarah said airily as she opened the door to her living room. This was not true. She had – actually only briefly – fondled 'Sharlz's' penis within his trousers and underpants, just as he had, equally briefly, touched her breasts inside two layers of clothing. Nevertheless she thought that tonight would be the ideal opportunity to drop her bombshell on Ruth.

'I expect I shall go all the way with him now,' she began in a casual tone, sprawling on the floor beside the record player. Ruth stood over her.

'Sarah! You *mustn't*! Imagine if you got pregnant.'

'Well, it's safe at the moment.' Sarah's sexual knowledge, like that of most public-school-educated girls of her age, was a sketchy combination of animal biology and cloakroom gossip, short on technical detail, but she hoped she knew the bare bones of what was essential. 'Anyway, I can always get him to wear one of those – you know – rubber johnnies.'

'Yuck,' said Ruth. 'I'm going to wait till I get married. Don't *you* want to be a virgin on your wedding night?'

Sarah let go her bombshell. 'Too late for that,' she said with considered nonchalance, thumbing through her LP collection.

'*Sarah*! You *haven't*!' Ruth's spots now stood out like studs. She sat down on the floor beside Sarah. '*When* did you – *where* did you – *who with*?'

'Two nights ago, in my car, in the woods.'

'With that awful motorbike chap?'

'With Malcolm.'

'Malcolm *Davison*?' One of their tennis crowd, a gangly youth with worse acne than Ruth.

'No, silly. Malcolm that was staying here with the motorbike chap. Malcolm who kissed you in the hospital.' She continued to leaf through records. Her tone added: Malcolm who *kissed you*, but *fucked me*. Ruth looked dejected, but her curiosity got the better of her:

'What was it like? Does it hurt?'

Sarah settled for a Johnny Mathis LP that would get her in a smoochy mood for Carlo. 'A bit. The first time.'

'How many times did you do it?'

Sarah removed Johnny Mathis from his sleeve and set him onto the spindle of the gramophone. Her most effective lies, like her sins (prior to Thursday), were those of omission rather than those of commission. As the needle began to hiss on the record she took refuge in a line she'd used on 'the motorbike chap':

'That's for me to know and for you to find out.'

DOWNSTAIRS LAURENCE, WITH an effort, buttressed Andrew's attempts to keep the atmosphere light. He almost suggested they go to the television room and watch the news at 8.45, but even Evelyn seemed to have forgotten the Caribbean crisis. Then she stood up to go to bed.

'I'll come up with you,' Laurence said. 'Make sure the girls haven't got the music on too loud. And I promised to call my ex-wife back.' He had no intention of phoning Louise tonight and was trying to leave Andrew alone with David. After the 'ordeal' with Pilgrim Andrew might benefit from a few minutes in the company of his lost teenage lover. Laurence hoped he could trust him not to make any unwelcome advances on David, whom marriage seemed to have stabilized in a way that it had not stabilized Laurence.

'Ruth and I ought to get going,' said David, but he didn't rise from the settee. Andrew, at a rare loss for words, offered cigarettes as the door closed behind Evelyn and Laurence. David shook his head.

'Andy, can I ask you something?'

'Anything you like, *Dave*,' Andrew said expansively, lighting his cigarette.

'You and Mr Dickinson – and this Italian fellow – you're all bisexual, aren't you? Forgive me if I'm wrong. And forgive me if I'm going too far.'

'You're not going too far.' Andrew's calm response belied his astonishment at the question. 'And you're not wrong. I may have underestimated you, David. How did you know? Surely it's not something we wear on our sleeves? Or are you a member of our little "fraternity"?'

David shook his head. 'No, I'm not, but in my work I come across a lot of men who are, as well as a lot more who are simply – homosexuals. You gave the game away the other day when you reminded me of what we did when we were at school. I'm not going to pretend I've forgotten it, but it doesn't seem all that important to me, whereas it's obviously something you still think about a lot.'

Andrew's hand shook as he brought his cigarette to his mouth. He managed to smile. 'Tell me how you fitted Laurence and Carlo into the jigsaw.'

'Ruth reminded me about you living here with Mr Dickinson some years ago, and now this chap who looks like a gigolo has turned up to be his driver.'

Andrew feigned applause and then had to brush ash off the arm of the chair he'd taken over from Evelyn. 'So – are you going to tell your sister not to come anywhere near this "Den of Iniquity" after tonight?'

David shook his head again. 'Why would I do that? Sarah's her friend. And there's nothing here that threatens Ruth.'

'Very broadminded of you,' Andrew said, smiling to lessen the sarcasm.

David was not smiling. 'Don't mistake my broad-mindedness for tolerance. People like you spread diseases that can ruin other people's lives.'

'Diseases that keep you in a job!'

'Don't be flippant, Andy. Women catch diseases from bisexual men that can sterilize them if they're not treated in time.' He held up a hand to prevent Andrew from interrupting. 'I know what you're going to say: prostitutes are the biggest carriers of VD, and men who frequent prostitutes are just as likely to infect their wives. And yes, thanks to antibiotics we can treat these diseases, though I can tell you that some people who keep getting reinfected are beginning to develop a resistance to the drugs we use.'

Andrew decided that a joke about his own brushes with NSU and gonorrhoea might also be deemed 'flippant'.

'So, is that what bisexuals and homosexuals are to you – a load of "Typhoid Marys"?'

Another shake of the head. 'Not at all. I'm not a psychologist, but I know enough to realize that most people can't control these sorts of urges and desires, but it's all this rampant promiscuity that I see the consequences of which I find hard to accept. *I'm* happy with one person. My *wife* is. Why can't homosexual men settle down with one partner?'

'And bisexuals?'

'They need to make up their minds and settle down as well. Sorry if I sound like some tub-thumping Jehovah's Witness.'

'You do. You only see things in black and white. Since you have to deal with the "flotsam and jetsam" of human sexuality, I'd expect you to have a better understanding of the "grey areas" where some of us are forced to live.'

'Or where you *choose* to live.'

Andrew sighed. Discussion – argument – was futile. 'It's easy to talk about choice in your black-and-white world, but not where *I* live – in one of the grey areas.'

'But when I asked if you were *happy* the other day on my dad's boat, you only had a smart-alec answer. I'd *like* to see you happy, Andy. Maybe you could be if you moved out of this grey area of yours into my black-and-white one.'

This would have been a suitable point at which to tell David that he hoped to marry Evelyn. Why didn't he? Because he was unsure of her? Of himself? Because David's reaction might echo what he himself had said to Fiona five days ago: *'Older woman, younger man. That's a bit Somerset Maugham, wouldn't you say?'*

How strange it was that David, in his blazer and cricket flannels, looked so like the David he had loved and yet was such a different person. '*You* made me happy for a few years,' Andrew said. 'It seemed as simple as black-and-white then: the only time in my life when I think I've actually *been* happy.'

David was crestfallen for a moment. 'Maybe *I* was happy then too,' he said, offering Andrew a crumb of solace before as quickly taking it back. 'But I'm not the boy I was then, Andy.' If he intended to say more, he didn't. Andrew said it for him:

'Whereas I still am? I'm a sort of – Peter Pan who never grew up?' Perceiving how near the truth this was, he almost smiled and went into his Noël Coward routine. Then disappointment and impatience got the better of him.

'Go home, David. Go home to your wife and your cosy black-and-white world. Don't worry about me. I'll find my own road to Heaven or to Hell.' He wished he hadn't said this; if he said it to Algie, his partner would laugh and ask which *black-and-white* Joan Crawford melodrama it was lifted from.

'I hope we can still be friends,' David said, rising from his chair.

I wish we could still be lovers, Andrew almost said, and then he realized that this was no longer true. David had outgrown him and now – finally – he had outgrown the dream that was David.

'Of course,' he said automatically, knowing that their paths were unlikely to cross again and – almost – indifferent to the prospect.

Laurence opportunely chose this moment to re-enter the room, having verified that Carlo's light was out and having said goodnight to Mrs Danvers in her sitting-room before she put down her embroidery and went to bed.

WHILE LAURENCE SAW David and Ruth off, Andrew went to the library. Laurence joined him, carrying the brandy decanter. He poured generous measures into fresh glasses.

'I think I already know your tête-à-tête didn't go very well. Is he still being – what did you call him – "a stuffed shirt"?'

'He's practically ready for a soapbox on Hyde Park Corner!' Andrew managed a half-hearted laugh. 'Oh well, as my dad used to say if anyone got on the wrong side of him, "bugger him – and bugger all those who

don't bugger him".' His laugh turned bitter. 'Actually
that's the one thing I wish I'd done.'

'What?'

'Buggered him. David.'

'Welcome to the world of the disappointed,' said
Laurence who could, if he dwelt on it, divide the hand-
ful of men he'd been close to into those (really only
Derek) he wished he had buggered and those (three,
including Andrew) he wished he hadn't. 'Let it go,
Andrew. Let him go.'

'I don't have much choice, do I?' He drank most of
his brandy in a fierce gulp and coughed as the liquor
burned his throat. 'Let's talk about something else,' he
suggested hoarsely.

Removing a cigar tube, unpatriotically Cuban, from
his inside pocket, Laurence unscrewed it. 'All right.
Have you found out whether Pilgrim made some sort of
assault on Evelyn?'

'Yes I have, and yes he did. That's why she ran
home yesterday.'

The cigar cutter pressed painfully into Laurence's
hand as he balled it into a fist. 'God, if it hadn't been for
Malcolm … I should have given them some money and
put them in a boarding house. Even in my hotel. How
bad was it – what he did to her?'

'She can't bring herself to tell me. Something more,
I suspect, than what Sarah says he did with her and a
bit less, I hope, than what he did to me. Her reaction
may have been more than the event warranted.'

Lighting his cigar, Laurence belched clouds of
smoke. 'She's very subdued tonight. Is that Pilgrim's
fault or Khrushchev's?'

'It may be more my fault than either of them.'

'Why, what have you done?'

'Oh' – Andrew made an airy gesture with his hand –
'I took a leaf from D. H. Lawrence and fucked her in the
woods at Mayfield this afternoon.'

'Good God, Andrew! What on earth were you thinking of?'

'I was trying to superimpose something rather more
pleasurable over whatever Pilgrim had done. Evelyn's
led a very sheltered life, sexually. I'm betraying con-
fidences here, but she'd never experienced an orgasm
and now, thanks to me, she has.' His smile became a
self-satisfied smirk.

'What's so God-almighty important about that?'
Laurence demanded. 'So far as I recall, Louise never
had one either. She probably thought about shopping
or divorce while I was – making love to her. Don't you
see what you've done? You've given Evelyn a taste of
something her poor husband obviously can't match,
since he hasn't done so already. You've condemned
her to a life twice as unfulfilled as it was before.'

'I intend to take charge of her in that area.'

'What – by adding her to your catalogue of part-
time mistresses?'

'By marrying her.'

Laurence burst out laughing. 'Of course you're not
serious.'

'I assure you I am.'

'But – why Evelyn?'

'Because it's taken me three years to get to the
point with her that I usually reach in about three days
with a girl, that I sometimes used to reach in three
minutes with – men.' He swirled his brandy glass and
drank some. 'Because I can see how much she would
complete my life rather than just complement it. Because for the first time since – God help me, since
David – I care about somebody else more than I care
about myself.'

Laurence had not seen such naked honesty on
Andrew's face since their uneasy sexual liaison ended
with him moving to London three years ago. He tried
not to sound carping or envious as he replied:

'Andrew, I don't know what to say. I've always wanted the best for you. I have to admit I've never believed in this "conversion" of yours. I always thought you were running away from something that was bound to catch up with you in the end. That's what happened to me and, as you've reminded me this week, I never went a fraction of the distance into the – the "Queer World" – that you did. For me that world is always there, even though I do no more than get my hopes up a bit from time to time, like this summer with Carlo. I still think that's where you belong and that that's where your best chance of happiness lies.'

'But' – another naked emotion: was it desperation? – was stamped on Andrew's features – 'you've never found it there.'

Laurence shook his head. 'Yes I have. I saw what it could be, in the navy, in the war, with Derek, and then I found it again with you.' His face burned with embarrassment. These were not the kind of words they had exchanged three years ago, when Laurence had held back from making emotional demands for fear of driving away a lover half his age who was, he knew, only using him to escape from his stifling family and take a few steps further down the world of men who hunted men. 'I know it didn't work out, but it was there.'

It was Andrew's turn to look uncomfortable. 'Laurence, we're talking about *love* here, are we not? I've always known that what you felt for me was – deeper than what I felt for you, just as something that meant the world to me at school with David he only remembers as a bit of boyish messing about. I know the "Queer World"' – his intonation supplied quotation marks – 'is always going to cast a shadow over my life and maybe you're right, that's where I properly belong, but Evelyn's the best thing that's happened to me since I turned and walked away from – what I used to be. I'm hoping that wanting to make *her* happy will be enough to make *me* happy.'

Laurence felt close to tears. 'W*anting* happiness, especially for somebody else, puts you at least halfway to finding it,' he said. He picked up his brandy glass and drained it.

'Bedtime, I think.' His voice rasped with raw liquor and cigar smoke.

WHAT TO WEAR for her next step down the sexual road?

Sarah had resolved to stake her claim on Carlo's bed (it was an effort not to think of him, still, as 'Sharlz') as soon as everyone else was in theirs. The right outfit to be screwed in (or to be stripped of prior to being screwed) was as important as what you wore to be picked up in. She normally slept in pyjamas and had a selection ranging from babyish teddy-bears to masculine stripes. She also had a few nightdresses, but none that were erotically sheer or low-cut. Finally she settled on a plain white cotton nightie from Marks & Spencer with the minimum of frills at its demure neckline. Its nunlike modesty over her infuriatingly small breasts gave her some allure, she hoped, and it would allow Carlo more immediate access than pyjamas. She wore nothing underneath it.

Thus attired in what Pilgrim might have called a 'shagging shift', and barefoot, Sarah crept along the landing a few minutes after she heard her father's and Andrew's muffled voices on the stairs. The aroma of a Havana cigar hung in the air. Carlo's door was now encouragingly ajar and – Sarah's heart began to race with anticipation – his light was on, heliographing his availability. Then, just before she arrived at the door, beyond which lay her full flowering into ripe lascivious womanhood, she heard Andrew, within the room, say:

'From what I hear, you're a man of many parts.'

'Excuse me?' Sarah pictured Carlo's furrowed

brow.

'*Chauffeur, maître-d'hôtel, secrétaire, chanteur. Et quoi encore?*' This was within the limits of Benenden French, but Carlo's reply was incomprehensible:

'*J'ai fait tout ce qu'il fallait faire pour survivre.*'

Sarah was not the only horse stumbling at the language barrier. 'Can we play an English game that I can join in?' her father said.

'Sorry,' Carlo and Andrew said in unison. There was only one chair in the room that had been Malcolm's. Sarah wondered who was sitting on the bed. Should she peek round the door jamb? But how would she explain herself if challenged? Better to wait half an hour and try again. As she tiptoed back along the landing, Sarah noticed that light also showed at the bottom of Mrs Hunter's door.

EVELYN TOO HAD agonized – again – over what to wear. In her case the choice was limited to two nightdresses, one more frivolous than the other but neither of them exactly racy. Or should she open the curtains and lie naked on the bed in the moonlight? (Was there moonlight?) Lacking Sarah's resolution, Evelyn lay on her bed still wearing the red silk dress.

One part of her waited for Andrew to come to her, as she supposed he would after everyone went to bed, while another part contemplated closing her suitcase – she had only unpacked her toilet bag and the ensemble she'd changed into for dinner – and stealing away to London again. Would Sid see on her face that she was, doubly, an adulteress? Her mother, she was sure, would have seen it.

Alone, she blushed as she reviewed in clinical detail the orgasm she had waited thirty-six years to experience. It was perhaps less than *Lady Chatterley's Lover* had led her to expect, and yet it felt like so much more. With practice no doubt Andrew would lead her through all of Constance Chatterley's heavings and surgings and billowings.

But it wasn't only the sex. Andrew wanted her to divorce Sid and marry him! He loved her, evidently. And she, of course, had been slowly falling in love with him over the past three years.

It would ruin Sid's life. Or perhaps he would get over it. Evelyn thought that she would get over her guilt quite quickly, especially if she and Andrew went to live somewhere exotic. Almost anywhere would be more exotic than Hampstead Garden Suburb. Living there, it was no wonder she'd never had an orgasm. Women in Kensington and Paris and Marrakech probably had them all the time.

On the edge of sleep, lying in her red dress on the blue bed in the blue room, Evelyn wished that Andrew would come to her now, quickly, before she allowed her drifting life to drift her back to Sid.

'I THINK HE'S DROPPED off,' said Laurence.

'Was I boring him?' Andrew asked, laughing. They had followed Carlo into his room after encountering him coming out of the bathroom. Now they quietly left him, Andrew to his Moorish attic, Laurence to his bedroom facing the stairs.

There was an ashtray on Laurence's window ledge. He knocked the ash off his cigar and took another puff as he opened the curtains. Far offshore the lightship's horn sounded less like a fog warning than a summons to some maritime requiem. Fog crept up to the edge of the terrace; in the light from the first-floor rooms it seethed like a living entity.

Bright light shone from the room over the garage which should have been in darkness. And within the room there was movement.

As on Tuesday the window above the garage was open to the dank night air. Tonight Pilgrim was not sitting there with his feet up, masturbating in full view of the house. Tonight, still whitely naked, he stood in the middle of the room, brutally sodomizing Malcolm who was sideways to the window, bent half forward, legs apart and similarly naked, his mouth a silent rictus of pain. Pilgrim's eyes locked on Laurence, twenty yards away at his own window. His lips parted in a feral, baleful grin.

Laurence cracked. He put his cigar on the edge of the ashtray and crossed to the wardrobe where he kept his shotgun. Loading it from a box of shells on the top shelf, he went back to the window, raised the sash and leaned out. Pilgrim, pounding at Malcolm's bent-over body, saw the gun. He gave another malign leer and continued to pump violently between the younger boy's pale slender buttocks.

Laurence squeezed the trigger. The roar of the 12-gauge's discharge was instantly followed by the rattle of lead shot against the garage wall. Some of the pellets clearly entered the open first-floor window. The light bulb above Pilgrim and Malcolm shattered, plunging the room into darkness.

After reloading the shotgun Laurence walked calmly through his room and out onto the landing. Like characters in a French farce, his guests and fellow residents appeared in their doorways in various stages of undress and showing varying degrees of agitation.

Sarah, wearing a shift of conventual purity in place of her usual pyjamas, said:

'God, Laurence, I thought you'd blown your brains out. I've already started spending your money on Sharlz!'

Carlo, in his underpants, dishevelled and bleary-eyed, murmured:

'Qu'est-ce qui se passe? C'est la guerre ou quoi?'

Andrew, almost at the foot of the attic staircase, had not yet undressed; his unbuttoned shirt revealed a chest that Laurence had once worshipped but which now seemed scrawny in comparison to Carlo's honed physique. Taking his cue from the Italian, he smiled and said:

'Is this it? Are the Soviets on the beaches of Bexhill?'

Mrs Danvers, at the opposite end of the landing from Sarah, clutched her cat to her dressing-gowned chest. Her hair, unbunned, hung incongruously like a girl's. She took Andrew's contribution as factual rather than fatuous.

'What did I tell you, Mr Dickinson? Oh dear God, it's the end of the world.'

Evelyn, despite retiring more than an hour ago, was fully dressed except for her shoes. She said nothing, although her face, still made-up, radiated anxiety.

Laurence took the opportunity to get a word in:

'We haven't been invaded. Well' – he laughed mirthlessly – 'I suppose we have, but not by the Russians. It's just a couple of intruders over the garage.'

'Anyone we know?' Andrew asked. Laurence nodded.

'Our travellers – our "pilgrims", I should say – are back with us.' This elicited a new range of expressions: puzzlement from Carlo; annoyance from Sarah; concern from Mrs Danvers; amusement from Andrew; and something close to panic from Evelyn.

'I know they've somewhat abused your hospitality,' Andrew said, still smiling, 'but isn't your retribution a shade drastic, not to say beyond the law?'

'I'll explain later,' said Laurence curtly, and he headed for the stairs. 'Go back to bed, everybody.'

Carlo, and then Sarah, obeyed this instruction, closing their doors. The housekeeper's cat jumped from her arms and she followed it back into her living room, leaving the door open. Andrew and Evelyn remained where they were, Andrew looking quizzical while she had a cornered expression which he had seen before.

'Don't worry, darling. We've got a guard who's armed and clearly dangerous!'

IN LAURENCE'S BEDROOM a gust of wind blew his cigar off the edge of the ashtray. Still glowing, it rolled along the window ledge and came to rest against the loose-lined velvet curtains. The lining began to smoulder.

GLASS FROM THE shattered lightbulb crunched beneath Laurence's feet as he walked across the carpet and turned on the bedside lamp to add to the glow from the light over the stairs. With or without illumination the room remained empty. How – and where – could they have disappeared, naked, in the two or three minutes since he fired the shotgun? He had neither seen nor heard a motorcycle as he came from the house to the garage. And the room did not appear to have been occupied since Mrs Danvers hoovered and dusted and remade the bed in the wake of yesterday's unannounced departures. Their return and re-departure had left no mark. Except for the open window, the glass fragments on the floor and some lead shot on the bedspread Laurence might have hallucinated the entire incident.

He walked to the window to check the reverse view of his bestial vision. A different light seemed to be dancing in the fog that now shrouded the house itself. Then he realized what this light was: his bedroom curtains – and the window frame – were on fire.

'SOMETHING'S BURNING,' SAID Evelyn, her first words since the gunshot drew her fearfully to her bedroom door.

Andrew sniffed. 'You're right.' He opened the door

to Laurence's room at the same moment that Laurence, shouting 'FIRE!' at the top of his voice, re-opened the front door. In the through-draught between the downstairs hall and the open first-floor window the room erupted into an inferno. Heat seared Andrew in the seconds before he slammed the door shut.

'Christ Almighty,' he said. 'Get out, Evelyn. Get out now.'

Sarah and the housekeeper reappeared in their doorways as Laurence, puffing and shouting, reached the top of the stairs.

'Don't open your door,' Andrew cautioned him, 'or you'll kill us all. I think evacuation is the order of the day.'

'Downstairs, everybody,' Laurence ordered, still panting but now calm in the face of the havoc his impetuosity had wrought. 'Andrew, get Carlo out. I'll call the fire brigade.' He turned and descended the stairs.

While Andrew ran into Carlo's room, the three females disregarded Laurence's instructions and darted back into their own rooms. Sarah was the first to re-emerge, still barefoot and in her nightdress but clutching a bundle of her cherished 'pop' 45s. Next came Mrs Danvers who'd retrieved her cat and her handbag. Then, as Andrew pushed the sluggish Carlo out of his room and followed him with some of the younger man's discarded clothes, Evelyn came out of her room whose wall adjoining Laurence's was creaking ominously. She had put on her shoes and was carrying her suitcase, make-up bag and fur coat; she might have been a hotel guest routinely checking out.

'Evelyn, for God's sake!' said Andrew. He relieved her of the suitcase, dropping most of Carlo's belongings in the process, and nudged her ahead of him down the stairs behind the near-naked Italian as Laurence's bedroom door began to buckle.

BY THE TIME the fire brigade arrived, twenty minutes later, the fire had a fatal hold on the house. Most of the first floor was burning. The dormer windows of Andrew's attic room had exploded; roof tiles cracked like more gunshots. Evelyn had moved her Renault into the road, and Laurence had moved the Bentley, using a spare set of keys from the telephone table; but there were no spare keys to Sarah's Morris, onto which sparks and tile fragments were showering.

The firemen shooed Laurence and his guests back into the road where an audience of neighbours and passing motorists was gathering. The Dickinson party formed an incongruous group: from Evelyn in her mink coat and court shoes to Sarah in tennis shoes and a duffel coat salvaged from the hall closet. Carlo was wearing Laurence's warmest tweed coat over his own trousers and a pair of wellingtons. Mrs Danvers wore slippers and another of her employer's overcoats; her cat's head protruded from Sarah's tennis bag which it was sharing with the precious 45s. Andrew sported his Burberry over his now refastened shirt, Laurence – over his smoking jacket – an old raincoat he kept for bad-weather gardening.

With a crash that reminded Laurence of the Blitz and then, inevitably, of burning ships in the Atlantic, the centre section of the house collapsed, Andrew's Moorish attic tumbling into Laurence's bedroom whose floor in turn gave way and fell through to the drawing room. The shroud of fog retreated as flames roared through the gaping hole in the roof.

'Where are our two intruders?' Andrew asked Laurence as Evelyn walked back towards her car.

'I don't know. They've vanished again.'

'God help them if they're in the house,' Andrew said. 'You haven't explained why you fired at them.'

Laurence drew him away from the others. 'I looked out of my window and Pilgrim was – buggering

Malcolm in the room over the garage. They were both bollock naked, but when I got up there there was no sign that they'd been back at all. I'm not going mad, am I? Surely I couldn't have imagined it?'

Even with the house roaring and crackling in front of them, Andrew mustered a smile. 'Your imagination's always been *under*-active, Lorenzo old fruit. I think you'd better tell the firemen about them.'

'Should I? I suppose you're right. Anyway' – he turned back towards the others as the firemen began to play their hoses on the blazing house – 'we must get you all into shelter for the night. Carlo, you can take the Bentley and drive Andrew and Evelyn to my hotel in Hastings. Evelyn may want to follow you in her car. Andrew, you'll have to navigate. You'd better stay there too, Carlo. And you can drop Sarah off at Ruth's.'

'Why can't I go to the hotel?' Sarah demanded.

'Because you haven't got any clothes on. Ruth will have some things you can borrow.'

Sarah pulled a face at the prospect of wearing anything of Ruth's. 'Sharlz has lost everything except his trousers as well,' she pointed out. Carlo echoed this concern:

'Signor Lorenzo, I cannot go into a hotel dressed like this.'

'Well, you'll have to,' Laurence said. His house was burning down and these young people were worried about their appearance!

'We could stop off at my parents' house,' Andrew suggested. 'Some of my clothes from student days are still there.'

'There you are, then,' said Laurence. 'Olive, we'll see if one of the neighbours can put you up, so that your cat stays in familiar territory.'

'What about you?' Andrew asked.

'Well, obviously I'm not leaving here until the fire's out.' So far the flames were showing no retreat in the face of the hoses. He wondered if any of his pictures or the treasures in his library would survive the assault of fire and water. 'The neighbours will offer me a bed, I'm sure,' he went on. 'You'd better go and tell your lady-friend what's been decided.'

EVELYN WAS SITTING inside the Renault. She wound the window down as Andrew approached.

'Are you all right?' he asked. She nodded.

'Yes. Have they found – *them*?'

'Not yet. Laurence is telling the firemen about them now.'

'I hope Malcolm's safe but – the other one can burn in Hell for all I care,' she said savagely. Andrew decided to ignore this and concentrate on practicalities.

'We're going to drop Sarah off at the Yates's in Laurence's car and go to my parents' house to pick up some clothes for Carlo, and then we can all stay at Laurence's hotel in Hastings. Are you OK to follow us in your car, unless you want to leave it here and ride in the Bentley?'

Evelyn took only seconds to reply. 'If you don't mind, I'd rather go back to London.'

'I can't leave Laurence in the lurch,' Andrew said. 'Let's at least stay and see what the overall damage is. Go back tomorrow as planned.'

'You should probably stay,' she agreed. 'But I'll only be in the way.'

Andrew sighed. 'So – you've decided? It's back to Hampstead Garden, is it? Back to Sid.'

She looked down at the steering wheel. 'Andrew, what you asked me – I can't just – I need more time.'

He shook his head. 'No you don't, Evelyn. I'm not saying that my offer is "for one day only", as we say in the retail trade, but I think your answer to it needs to be – now or never.'

'I'm just no good at impetuous decisions,' she said.

She lifted her head and looked at him. He expected to see tears in her eyes, but there were none. 'How will you get home tomorrow?'

'I can go up on the train,' he said.

'Are you all right for money?'

'Actually, my wallet's in there – and my flat keys. But I can get some money from Laurence. And Algie's got my spare keys.'

Evelyn turned on the ignition. The Renault came smoothly to life. 'I'll get going now,' she said, 'if you don't mind.'

'If I mind!' he echoed with a laugh. He looked down at her in her red silk dress and mink coat: an auburn-haired woman whose carmine lipstick was almost but not quite daring; a woman who might have changed his life but who lacked the will to change her own – going home, now, to her husband.

'I'm sorry,' she said. 'I – I ...' She broke off, not knowing what to say or perhaps incapable of saying anything. 'I'm sorry,' she said again and drove off, belatedly remembering to turn the lights on.

Andrew turned back towards the others. Carlo, Sarah and Mrs Danvers with her sports-bagged cat remained grouped together in their assortment of coats and footwear. Laurence, in his gaberdine gardening coat, was a little forward of them, talking to one of the firemen. Behind him smoke and steam rose in roiling clouds from the house, blending with the fog to form an acrid-smelling smog.

Another section of the roof fell in, demolishing the rooms in which Evelyn, Malcolm and – briefly – Carlo had slept and, below these, the dining room, the entrance hall and the smaller sitting room in which they had watched some of the week's news on television.

SARAH RELUCTANTLY RODE in the rear of the Bentley with Andrew. Outside the Yates house she got out of the car with even greater reluctance.

'Can't I come with you?' she pleaded. Her eyes engulfed Carlo at the wheel.

'Better do what your father says,' said Andrew. They waited in the car while she rang the doorbell and stood there, a pretty teenager with long golden hair, wearing a duffel coat over a white nightdress and tennis shoes. David Yates came to the door, blond and beefy but no longer beguiling, in striped pyjamas.

'Let's go,' Andrew said.

EVELYN HEADED FOR Hastings and the A21. No side roads or country lanes for her: not tonight, and possibly never again.

Crawling through the fog along the seafront at St Leonards to where the A21 began, she suddenly recalled that she'd hung the lilac-and-grey chiffon dress in the wardrobe before dinner.

Well, it was gone now. She would have to buy it again, or perhaps something more suitable for a latter-day Lady Chatterley!

Still, Laurence had lost everything. All she'd lost was an 85-guinea frock.

Then why did she feel as if she'd lost everything too?

LILLIAN RUTHERFORD WAS still up, enjoying a library whodunnit in the quiet hour after putting her husband to bed. In a moment of perverseness Andrew introduced Carlo as 'Sharlz'. His mother was dazzled by the handsome young Frenchman in his comical wellingtons and borrowed overcoat. She would not hear of them going to a hotel and went to fetch sheets from the airing cupboard while Andrew took Carlo up to the loft where some of his old clothes were stored.

Kneeling on opposite sides of a cabin trunk bought for a cruise his parents had never taken, Andrew too felt dazzled by Carlo, naked to the waist, tanned and tousled.

'Laurence is not going to let you stay,' he said.

'Because of the fire?'

'Because of Sarah.'

'Ah.' Carlo nodded, then shrugged. '*Tant pis.*'

'*Mais vous pouvez venir avec moi. À Londres.*'

'*Vous avez besoin d'un chauffeur?*'

'*Peut-être. Et peut-être plus encore.*'

'*Ah, oui?*' Carlo, arching his eyebrows, didn't look in the least like Noël Coward – or even Maurice Chevalier. '*Mais je vous connais presque pas.*'

Andrew trawled his memory for an aphorism to bowdlerize and came up with: 'I am the *lust* that dare not speak its name.'

'I don't understand,' Carlo said. Understanding was not the point, Andrew thought: he wasn't sure that he understood himself. He leaned across and kissed the other on the mouth. Carlo was tense for a moment, then his lips parted and his tongue explored Andrew's mouth, deftly. Andrew ran his hands over the younger man's warm naked chest.

'Do you boys want hot-water-bottles in your beds?' Lillian called from the bottom of the loft ladder. Carlo's head sprang guiltily back. Andrew smiled into the dark-eyed wet-mouthed face across the open trunk.

'Us boys would love something to warm us up in bed,' he called back merrily to his mother.

LAURENCE GAZED AT what remained of his house, no longer ablaze but sparking and steaming as the firemen continued to hose the smouldering ruins. Mrs Danvers had been taken in by the family two doors away. The crowd of bystanders had thinned to a half-dozen.

The entire seaward side and most of the centre of the house were gutted. At the front Sarah's rooms, the

music room and Laurence's beloved library had survived the fire but he had not been allowed in to assess
the water damage. The kitchen appeared more or less
intact, as, ironically and infuriatingly, were the garage
and the room above it. Sarah's car, in front of the
garage, was scratched and dented from the rain of tiles
and window glass.

The fire chief allowed him to go nearer and loaned
him a flashlight. 'Just don't go anywhere inside, please,
sir,' he urged.

'I want to check on my greenhouses,' Laurence
replied.

His greenhouses were still standing but with much
of their glass shattered by flying debris. Laurence
walked to the edge of the terrace and played the flashlight on the charred and gaping wreckage of his home,
wreathed in fog like the skeleton of a beached ship.
Tears came, finally, to his eyes and he turned away,
still holding the flashlight whose powerful beam pierced
the fog blanketing the entire length of the garden and
revealed two dark-clad figures beneath the clifftop
gazebo.

'Hey, you two,' Laurence called and set out across
the slippery lawn, not knowing what he would find to
say to them when he got nearer. But before he was
more than halfway down the lawn the two black-
jacketed figures darted to the beach staircase, the
burly one ahead of the smaller one. Their feet clattered
on the rickety planking. Then, as Laurence reached the
cliff edge, the clattering gave way to splintering, crack-
ing sounds as the stanchions at the top of the stairs
parted and the entire structure tumbled onto the fallen
chalk and shingle.

Laurence shone the torch down the thirty feet of
cliff. Pilgrim was tugging at the pile of broken timbers
within which Malcolm's crushed and crumpled body
could be seen. As the beam of light touched him

Pilgrim looked up at Laurence. His dark eyes glittered malevolently and his mouth opened in an animal snarl. Laurence shuddered.

Then, a thicker coil of mist rolled in from the sea and engulfed the collapsed staircase. The flashlight's beam no longer penetrated the dense swirling fog.

'I'll get help,' Laurence shouted. He started back across the lawn, his feet slithering on the dank grass, his heart pounding in his chest.

THE HOUSES ON either side had given up their beach access in the interest of security. Laurence too had suffered attempted break-ins and occasional invasions of his gazebo and lawn by drunken nocturnal revellers. He directed the firemen to the house two doors away where Mrs Danvers was being sheltered, which had concrete steps to the beach.

But they found no sign of Malcolm and Pilgrim. Nor was there so much as a shred of clothing or a blood-stain in the pile of rubble at the base of Laurence's cliff.

SUNDAY

THE CUBAN MISSILE crisis ended at 11 a.m. Eastern Standard Time on Sunday October 28th when the Soviet Ambassador to Washington, Anatoly F. Dobrynin, went to the office of US Attorney General Robert F. Kennedy in the Justice Department building and informed him that Chairman Khrushchev agreed to dismantle and withdraw the offending missiles.

At a meeting the previous evening Robert Kennedy had told Dobrynin that, although his brother's latest ultimatum to Khrushchev did not admit the concession, NATO missile installations in Turkey would be reciprocally removed. In fact, these were obsolete silos whose dismantling the President had ordered two months earlier.

The Attorney General had emphasized that although the President's objective was peace, not war, any further shooting down of reconnaissance planes would meet with retaliation and the inevitable risk of escalation.

The term 'brinkmanship' would be employed to honour the Kennedy brothers' handling of this crisis, although some historians would argue that the true master of the game was Khrushchev.

BRITAIN'S SUNDAY NEWSPAPERS, having gone to press with Saturday's ominous developments, were the most doom-laden of the week. '**Kennedy: No deal till Cuban missiles are made useless**' was *The Observer*'s headline; '*The world is at stake,*' wrote the editor. A similar front page in the *Sunday Times* was followed up by a similar leader: '... *fading hopes of an* *armistice … time is running out rapidly.'*

The tabloids, as usual, were blunter – and had other fish to fry. '**AMERICA: NO**' headlined *The People,* which also printed revelations by a former butler to the Queen from the time when she and Prince Philip were newlyweds. After a cocktail party whose thirty guests included her father, King George VI, the then Princess Elizabeth asked the butler how many bottles of gin had been consumed.

The *News of the World* divided its front page between Cuba, under the headline '**KENNEDY SAYS NO**', and a follow-up to the week's other main story in Britain, the Vassall espionage trial. The paper reported a proposed MI5 investigation into the private lives of government workers; this would include a check on '*known haunts of homosexuals, particularly drinking clubs.'*

William Vassall, the homosexual Admiralty clerk blackmailed into spying for the Soviets, had been sentenced to eighteen years' imprisonment on Monday, the day the Missile Crisis entered the public domain. The *News of the World*'s cover story was followed up with an article headlined '**Twilight Creatures**'; the hapless clerk was described as '*a member of the Third Sex to whom the ordinary human values mean nothing.'* Another Admiralty employee was brought into the story: Norman Rickard, the victim of an unsolved murder, found strangled and naked in a cupboard of his Maida Vale flat. Rickard, the *News of the World* informed its famously prurient readers, had been given to wearing a leather jacket, blue jeans and '*high-heeled cowboy boots with silver buckles*' (the opportunity for a topical tie-in was missed: these boots were known as 'Cuban heels'); Rickard '*wandered round Marble Arch trying to make friends with other men.'*

Aptly perhaps, this had been the week in which

Katherine Anne Porter's epic and ponderously symbolic novel *Ship of Fools* was published in the UK. The *Sunday Times* gave it a rave review, although Angus Wilson, reviewing it for *The Observer*, made much of the fact that it had taken the authoress twenty years to write and found it to be '*only a very middling good sort of novel.*'

AS WHEN, THIRTEEN months later, John F. Kennedy was assassinated in Dallas, most people would remember for a long time where they were and what they were doing when they heard the news of the resolution of the Cuban crisis.

MRS DANVERS WAS the first member of the now scattered Dickinson household to hear the news. The kitchen radio was tuned to the Home Service in the house two doors away where she was helping her hostess prepare the evening meal.

'Glory be,' exclaimed the housekeeper. In her relief she crossed herself. Not being a Catholic, she did this back-to-front and upside-down. She hurried to tell her employer. But Laurence, having spent the day transferring sodden books and pictures into the room over the garage where he'd seen Pilgrim brutalizing Malcolm, was asleep on the bed below the boarded-up window.

Mrs Danvers decided that the glad tidings would keep till dinnertime.

IN HAMPSTEAD GARDEN SUBURB, Sidney Hunter was listening to the Light Programme while he caught up with the week's papers. He rushed up to the bedroom where his wife lay under the bedspread nursing a headache.

'Thank God,' said Evelyn. She felt like crying – she'd felt like crying all day – but she mustered a brave smile for Sidney: faithful Sid whom she had betrayed twice in forty-eight hours. She would, she knew, never forgive herself.

She tried not to think of Andrew. He had given her a gift which she'd felt unable to accept. She hoped she had not ruined his life as she had ruined Sid's and her own.

To her surprise she could now, almost, think of Pilgrim without wanting to be sick.

SARAH AND RUTH were listening to Sarah's 45s on a portable gramophone in Ruth's bedroom when David brought them the news from the television downstairs. 'Yippee!' cried Ruth.

Sarah said nothing. Her father had told her of his intention to give Carlo some money and send him away. She'd spent the day wondering what sexual adventures lay in store for her in Hawaii.

If she thought of Pilgrim it was only as, like 'Sharlz' and all too literally, another penis that had slipped through her fingers.

LILLIAN RUTHERFORD PUT the television on for George. The telephone rang just as she was about to pick it up and call Andrew in case he hadn't heard the news. He'd set off for London after breakfast, the young Frenchman still driving Laurence Dickinson's Bentley and looking like an English sixth-former in Andrew's old football jersey. Andrew had spent the night in his boyhood room, now the guestroom of which his sister and her husband were more frequent users than he was; 'Sharlz' had slept in Sylvia's old room which George had repainted in bright colours when their twin granddaughters were born.

'I was just going to call you,' Lillian said, but it wasn't Andrew on the phone.

'It must be telepathy,' replied Amy Sadler, whose husband had been Lillian's first 'beau' before she jilted him in favour of George. More urgent than the news from Washington, she wanted to tell Lillian the proceeds of yesterday's bazaar in aid of Moral Rearmament.

ANDREW IGNORED THE telephone when his mother rang at the end of her call from Amy Sadler and, again, later in the evening. He had been – and remained – almost continuously in bed with Carlo since they arrived in South Kensington after the detour to Richmond to collect the spare keys from Algie.

Not only was it the best sex he'd known in the last three years, it was the most complete sex he'd ever had. With Carlo Andrew experienced what he had failed to find with Fiona and the girls before her, the sensation he had hoped to bring into Evelyn's life: *transcendental* sex.

They didn't hear the news about Cuba until Monday morning.

WHERE, AND WHEN, Pilgrim and Malcolm heard it is, like everything else about them, unknown – perhaps unknowable.

'Imperialism today is no longer what it used to be when it held undivided sway over the world. If it is now a "paper tiger", those who say this know that this "paper tiger" has atomic teeth. It can use them and it must not be treated lightly.'

**Nikita S. Khrushchev,
addressing the Supreme Soviet,
12 December 1962**

* * *

'The week of the Cuban missile crisis … was the week of most strain I can ever remember in my life.'

**Harold Macmillan
addressing the House of Commons,
17 June 1963**

Acknowledgements

Heartfelt thanks to Rod Shelton for many hours of editorial advice and nursing me through the intricacies of fonts and formatting. Mike George shared his knowledge of shotguns. Michael Harth at Paradise Press provided valuable support and encouragement, as have the members of three writer groups: Sussex Authors, Southeast Authors and London's Gay Authors Workshop.

My research for the Cuban missile crisis consisted largely of reading the newspapers from October 1962. Of the historical accounts, the most succinct and the most valuable was *13 Days* by the late Robert F. Kennedy (Pan Books, 1969). RFK was the source of the letters quoted at the end of my chapters, which I gratefully acknowledge.

SHAIKH-DOWN

David Gee

A sassy American airhostess and a gay British banker help their Arab boyfriends kickstart a revolution on the island emirate of Belaj in the Persian Gulf. An Arab princess's life takes surprising turns before and after the coup, as does her brother's, the Emir's Chief of Security.

David Gee's 'Arab Spring' blueprint centres on the Emir's bedchamber and offers swifter, less brutal Regime Change than current events seem to predict for the region.

* * * * * * * * * * * * * * * *

'*Witty, entertaining, raunchy and very well written.*'

Peter O'Donnell, creator of *Modesty Blaise*

'*Ribald and politically incorrect. Set in a fictitious but absolutely believable Arab state where sheikhs and their minions are locked in a life-and-death struggle to survive the relentless move towards democracy. Entertaining.*'

GAY TIMES

'*Probably a Zionist plot masterminded by the CIA to undermine the good image of morally irreproachable Gulf Arabs.*'

GULF TIMES

* * * * * * * * * * * *

Available in paperback and as an e-book from bookshops, Amazon or www.paradisepress.org.uk

THE DROPOUT

David Gee

* * * * * * * *

Don't fall for Paul. He'll drive you to the edge.

* * * * * * * *

Looking for a woman to love, college dropout Paul makes some bad choices. And he has to learn how to handle unwelcome advances from gay admirers. In this new take on *The Graduate*, Paul's 'Mrs Robinson' turns out to be his 'Madame Bovary'.

* * * * * * * *

'David Gee's tongue-in-cheek, if dark, social and sexual satire (a sort of cross between David Lodge and Tom Sharpe) leads us through a topsy-turvy world of sexual shenanigans and unconventional relationships.'

POLARI MAGAZINE

* * * * * * * *

Available in paperback and as an e-book from bookshops, Amazon or www.paradisepress.org.uk

JASON HOWL:
The Road to Eldorado
David Gee

A blue-eyed hunk from the boondocks, Jason Howl is just another Los Angeles wannabe until some juicy footage on the internet turns him from a bit-part player in the nation's raunchiest soap into a superstar – and the hottest date in Hollywood.

* *

KATHARINE KANE:
A Star is Porn
David Gee

A sultry teenage belle from Louisiana, Joylene Duchat becomes Kate 'Pussy-Kat' Kane, the 'Beaver Queen' of Porno. After her 'legitimate' debut as Nell Gwynne in a British sex-romp, Kate is offered a big break by Isaac Hunt, one of the last independent studio heads.

* * * * * * * * * * * * * * * * *

coming in 2014,

**the first two parts of David Gee's new trilogy
spoofing every Hollywood book you've ever read
– from Nathaniel West to Jackie Collins!**

also from Paradise Press:

Bokassa's Last Apostle

Rod Shelton

Can Everton Jones discover how his father stole Emperor Bokassa's diamonds before his followers – his Apostles – get there first? Everton and his friends romp all over the gay scene in London to find out, fight a demon and run into a street war.

Finalist in the 2013 Lambda Literary Awards (USA).
ISBN 978 1 904585 41 1 £10.99.
Also available as an e-book.

Twenty-Two Eighty-Four

Christopher Preston

In 2284 AD; Utopia or dystopia? That depends on your gender and sexuality. Climate change and a fertility virus have transformed the world and women are now in charge. Pitto Kucera, the only son of a wealthy and powerful family of women, turns nineteen and begins to challenge his rôle in society.

ISBN 978 1 904585 62 6 £7.99.
Also available as an e-book.

IN PRINT FROM PARADISE PRESS:

(*also/†only available as an e-book for kindle and e-pub e-readers)

BEHIND THE MASK* by Winston Green (2011) 94pp. £3.99
ISBN 978 1 904585 17 6

THE BEST OF GAZEBO edited by Michael Harth (2012) 208pp. £7.99
ISBN 978 1 904585 47 3

THE BEXHILL MISSILE CRISIS* by David Gee (2014) 224pp. £7.99
ISBN 978 1 904585 59 6

BOKASSA'S LAST APOSTLE* by Rod Shelton (2012) 304pp. £10.99
ISBN 978 1 904585 41 1

THE CARRIER BAG* by John Dixon (2013) 198pp. £6.99
ISBN 978 1 904585 40 4

CAT TALISMAN† by Michael Harth (2014) £2.99 ISBN 978 1 904585 66 4

COCKSUCKERY† by Ian Stewart (2011) £2.99 ISBN 978 1 904585 25 1

COMING CLEAN edited by John. Dixon & Jeffrey Doorn (2014) 128pp.
£5.99 ISBN 978 1 904585 69 5

DREAM DEVICE† by Michael Harth (2014) £2.99
ISBN 978 1 904585 67 1

EROS AT LARGE – TALES OF DESIRE edited by Michael Harth (2013)
272pp. £8.99 ISBN 978 1 904585 46 6

FIRST AND FIFTIETH* by Martin Foreman (2002) 152pp. £6.99
ISBN 978 0 9525964 7 9

GAY LIFE, STRAIGHT WORK* by Donald West (2012) 236pp. £9.99
ISBN 978 1 904585 23 7

GHOSTS AND GARGOYLES by Elsa Wallace (2013) 144pp. £6.99
ISBN 978 1 904585 43 5

GURU ON HIRE† by Michael Harth (2013) £2.99
ISBN 978 1 904585 65 7

HOMO JIHAD by Timothy Graves (2010) 298pp. £8.99
ISBN 978 1 904585 15 2

MY LIFE OUTSIDE* by Elizabeth J. Lister (2012) 204pp. £7.99
ISBN 978 1 904585 37 4

A LIFE'S TALES* by Joseph Hucknall (2013) 240pp. £7.99
ISBN 978 1 904585 49 7

A LITTLE CHAT by Michael Harth (2003) 166pp. £6.99
ISBN 978 1 9045895 02 2

THE MONKEY MIRROR* by Elsa Wallace (2010) 142pp. £6.99
ISBN 978 1 904585 16 9

A NEW MAN IN OLD STEINE by Graham Robertson (2004) 204pp. £7.99
ISBN 978 0 9525964 1 7

NOTHING STAYS THE SAME* by Elizabeth J. Lister (2012) 224pp. £7.99
ISBN 978 1 904585 48 0

OYSTERS AND PEARLS edited by Jeffry Doorn & Adrian Risdon (2010)
88pp. stapled, card cover £3.99 ISBN 978 1 904585 13 8

PEOPLE YOUR MOTHER WARNED YOU ABOUT* edited by G. Abel-
Watters (2011) 254pp. £7.99 ISBN 978 1 904585 12 1

THE PHYSENT by Michael Harth (2003) 156pp. £6.99
ISBN 978 1 904585 03 9

THE PICNIC by Michael Harth (2002) 148pp. £6.99
ISBN 978 0 9525964 3 1

IVOR TREBY, POEMS 2007–2012 edited by John Dixon (2014) 192pp.
£7.99 ISBN 978 1 904585 70 1

PRISONER 537* by Elizabeth J. Lister (2012) 184pp. £7.99
ISBN 978 1 904585 24 4

QUEER HAUNTS edited by G. Abel-Watters (2nd Edn 2013) 198pp. £8.99
ISBN 978 1 904585 58 9

RID ENGLAND OF THIS PLAGUE by Rex Batten (2006) 320pp. £8.99
ISBN 978 1 904585 08 4

SEEKING, FINDING, LOSING by John Dixon (2011) 56pp. £3.99
ISBN 978 1 904585 18 3

A SHORT HISTORY OF LORD HYAENA† by Elsa Wallace (2012) £1.99
ISBN 978 1 904585 51 0

SLIVERS OF SILVER edited by Jeffrey Doorn & Adrian Risdon (2003)
60pp. £2.99 stapled, card cover ISBN 978 1 904585 05 3

TWENTY-TWO EIGHTY-FOUR* by Christopher Preston (2014) 304pp.
£7.99 ISBN 978 1 904585 62 6